PHOENIX

A WOLFES OF MANHATTAN NOVEL

HELEN HARDT

HARDT & SONS

PHOENIX

A WOLFES OF MANHATTAN NOVEL

Helen Hardt

WWW.HELENHARDT.COM

For Eric, my editor and son!

PRAISE FOR HELEN HARDT

"Helen Hardt is a master at making you fall for the bad boy."
    ~**Words We Love By** on *Savage Sin*

"Hardt spins erotic gold..."
    ~**Publishers Weekly** on *Follow Me Darkly*

"22 Best Erotic Novels to Read"
    ~**Marie Claire** Magazine on *Follow Me Darkly*

"Intensely erotic and wildly emotional..."
    ~**New York Times** bestselling author Lisa Renee Jones on
Follow Me Darkly

"With an edgy, enigmatic hero and loads of sexual tension,
Helen Hardt's fast-paced *Follow Me Darkly* had me turning
pages late into the night!"
    ~**New York Times** bestselling author J. Kenner on *Follow
Me Darkly*

"Christian, Gideon, and now…Braden Black."
    ~**Books, Wine, and Besties** on *Follow Me Darkly*

"This red-hot tale will have readers fanning themselves."
    ~**Publishers Weekly** on *Blush*

"Scintillating…"
    ~**Publishers Weekly** on *Bloom*

"An absolute must-read. With its engaging plot and enthralling characters, this novel keeps you hooked from start to finish."
    ~**The Llama Library** on *Bloom*

"Helen's intelligent writing style and skills have made this story a must-read."
    ~**FireSerene Reads** on *Bloom*

"It's hot, it's intense, and the plot starts off thick and had me completely spellbound from page one."
    ~**The Sassy Nerd Blog** on *Rebel*

"This book was fantastic! It was steamy, funny, romantic, and just about any other emotion you can think of…"
    ~**Steamy Book Mama** on *Lily and the Duke*

"The writing was fast paced and *hot* for a historical romance…with lots of chemistry…and a lot of fun!
    ~**Bound by Books** on *Lily and the Duke*

"Craving is the jaw-dropping book you *need* to read!"

WOLFES OF MANHATTAN READING ORDER

Rebel

Recluse

Runaway

Rake

Reckoning

Escape

Moonstone

Raven

Garnet

Buck

Opal

Phoenix

Amethyst

WARNING

This book contains adult language and scenes, including flashbacks of physical and sexual abuse. Please take note.

PROLOGUE

LEIF

Kelly stares down at her lap, her hands clasped together. Is she thinking? Is she getting ready to strike?

I don't think she's getting ready to strike because she doesn't think before doing that. If she were going to strike again, she would've already done so.

Then the ding of a text.

Kelly reaches for her small purse and pulls out her cell phone.

Then she gasps.

"What is it?"

"Another one." She hands the phone to me.

You will get what you deserve, you traitorous bitch.

"You're truly off the hook now, Brindley," Leif says.

"Oh my God, is it another one of those texts?" Brindley asks.

I nod, and Kelly stays quiet.

"I'm sorry you got this," I say. "But I swear to God I will protect you. And now... Do you believe that it's not Brindley?"

"Why should I? She could have someone sending them for her."

I sigh. "Kelly... Please."

Finally, she looks up at me, her gorgeous eyes laced with sadness. "Who's doing this to me, Leif? Who? And why?"

"I don't know, baby. But I swear to God we will find out." I turn back to Brindley. "I'm sorry we bothered you."

"It was no bother. I'm happy to have any kind of chance to prove my innocence. I guess it doesn't matter now. Whoever texted Kelly proved it for me."

"Kelly?" I say.

She looks to Brindley. "It's not you, is it?"

"No, it's not. It never was."

I don't expect Kelly to apologize to Brindley, so I rise and offer her my hand. "You want to go home?"

"Yeah." She stands as well, and then she turns to Brindley. "I... I'm sorry."

Brindley drops her jaw.

And I keep from dropping mine.

"I'm just glad my name has been cleared," Brindley says. "I do hope you find out who's doing this to you, Kelly. You don't deserve it. None of us deserves any more pain for the rest of our lives."

Kelly simply nods, and then she walks toward the door. I follow her.

"Thank you for your hospitality, Brindley."

"Any time. Both of you are always welcome here. I get kind of lonely."

"Will you be returning to your family soon?" I ask.

"Sadly, I don't have a family," Brindley says. "I grew up in the foster system. I got kicked out of that when I was eighteen, so with no place to go, I ended up on the streets. In a bizarre way, the island saved me. At least I got enough to eat every day."

Kelly drops her jaw. "I didn't know."

"You didn't ask me."

"You've never talked about it in group therapy," Kelly says.

"You've never talked about your childhood in group therapy either."

Kelly closes her mouth then.

"I'm sorry to hear about that," I say to Brindley. "If you need anything, I'm in the apartment next to Kelly's."

"That's kind of you, but the Wolfe family has made sure I have everything I need. And Macy is a wonderful therapist. To be honest, this is the best home I've ever had. I'm not in any hurry to leave it. Good night."

She closes the door, leaving Kelly and me in the hall.

"I didn't know," Kelly says.

"I know you didn't. Everyone has a story. Everyone is so much more than what they seem on the surface. You are way more than what you seem on the surface, Kelly. Deep down inside you are an amazing person, and I hope one day you see that."

Her lips tremble. "Why are you so nice to me?"

I open my mouth, but she interrupts me.

"It's your job, isn't it?"

"My job is to protect you, baby. Nothing in the job description says I need to be nice to do that."

That actually gets a smile out of her.

But then she looks at her phone, and the sadness returns.

"I don't understand," she says. "Who could be doing this?"

The elevator dings then, and we get on and go down to the fourth floor.

Kelly's phone dings again.

Her lips tremble. "I'm almost afraid to look."

I take the phone from her.

And I widen my eyes as my heart nearly beats right out of my chest.

"What?" Kelly demands. "What is it?"

I love you.

The words don't come out, but I feel them more than ever...along with a raw instinct to protect her. And to take out whoever's threatening her.

Because this last text?

Whoever sent it means business.

1

KELLY

"It's nothing," Leif says. "Just some spam."

I hold out my hand. "Give me the phone."

He taps on it a few times and then hands it back to me. The last text is the one I've already seen.

You will get what you deserve, you traitorous bitch.

Anger crawls up the back of my neck. "You fucking erased it!"

Brindley opens the door again. "Everything all right out here?"

"Yes. Fine." Leif walks back into Brindley's apartment. "I'm sorry about this, Brindley."

I shake my head. "I can't believe you erased my text."

"No," Leif says calmly. "I forwarded it to my phone, and then I deleted it from yours."

"The message was for me," I grit out.

"Kelly..."

"What did it say, Leif? Give me your damned phone."

Brindley's eyes are wide, and her lips tremble slightly. "What did it say?" she asks softly.

"That's none of your fucking business, is it?" I whip my hands to my hips. "You're not sending these texts after all, so none of this has anything to do with you."

Leif sighs. "Come on, Kelly. There's no reason to treat her that way."

Leif is right, of course. I hate it when Leif is right. Because right now I'm angry, and I'm not angry with Brindley. I'm angry with Leif. And with myself. No matter how hard I try, I end up regressing to my old ways. I strike out. I lash out. I spew nasty words. Nasty words that I want to take back.

And then I'm forced to apologize, and apologizing is so difficult for me.

But an apology isn't what's first on my mind. It's the text—the text Leif won't let me see.

"Why?" I demand. "Why did you delete it?"

"You know why, Kelly."

"No, I really don't."

"To protect you."

"Right." I scoff. "Because protecting me is your *job*."

Brindley's gaze darts from me, to Leif, to me again. Her eyes are wide, her lips still trembling. She's frightened. Brindley is frightened for me.

As I regard her, I wonder how I ever could have thought she was behind this. She's so young. I'd say naïve, except that anyone who spent any time on that island knows way too much about the world to be considered naïve.

But her freckled face... Her round cheeks... Damn. She's still just a girl.

I'd feel for her if I weren't so damned mad.

"Let's go, Kelly," Leif says.

"Oh, hell, no. I'm done taking orders from you."

Leif comes close to me, speaks low in my ear. "Look at Brindley. You've got her so freaked out."

"I've got *her* so freaked out? You're the one who won't tell me what the text said."

"Brindley," Leif says, "I'm very sorry for all that we've put you through. You're clearly exonerated now, as the last text came through while we were sitting here."

"She could've had someone somewhere else texting for her." I curl my hands into fists.

"Kelly, come on." Leif shakes his head. "You just said you believed it wasn't her."

Again, I'm lashing out. I don't believe Brindley is behind the texts. I convinced myself of it because to think otherwise would mean I didn't know. And that's much scarier.

"Let's go," he says.

"Maybe I'm not ready to go."

"I'm so sorry, Brindley." Leif takes my hand.

I yank it away. He's a broken record. How many times is he going to tell Brindley he's sorry?

"Kelly... Come on..."

"I said I'm not ready to leave. Not until you show me the text."

"This has nothing to do with Brindley. We need to leave her out of this."

Anger envelops me. I feel like I'm going to explode in rage.

But who am I truly angry at?

At Brindley? No. Look at her. She's hardly out of her teens. She's the girl next door, and in my heart I know she wouldn't hurt a fly.

Is it Leif?

Yes and no. Yes, I'm angry because he deleted my text. But I also know he's doing it to protect me. How can I be angry at that?

Easy. I don't need protection.

Except maybe I do.

My life has been hell. Hell for so long. First from my mother, and then on the island.

The best part of my life was the five years I waited tables in Phoenix. I always wondered if my mother would come after me, but she never did. As I look back now...why would she? She's the one who kicked me out. She was glad to be rid of me.

I'm tired of being so angry. It's exhausting, and the fact of the matter is... I've been a lot less angry since Leif came into my life.

That's got to mean something, right?

I already apologized to Brindley, but I'm not sure she believed me the first time, so I turn. "I'm sorry," I say, in almost a whisper. "I'm sorry, Brindley." Then I let Leif lead me out of her apartment.

"I'm glad you apologized to her," he says.

I scoff. "It's not your business to be glad of anything that I do."

He rubs his jawline, shaking his head. "Kelly, why do you always have to make everything so hard? I'm telling you that you did a nice thing. I know how angry you are right now, and you took the time to be nice to a woman who you thought for so long was your enemy. Take it for what it is. A compliment."

"I don't need compliments from you, Leif."

"What *do* you need, Kelly?"

"From you?"

"From anyone." He lets out a heavy sigh. "For God's sake, we've been intimate, Kelly. It was damned good, and from all evidence that I saw, it was good for you too."

"Stop using that silly euphemism, Leif." I roll my eyes. "There was nothing *intimate* about what we did. We didn't make love. We fucked."

"Maybe that's all it was to you," he says.

We reach the elevator, and the doors are already open. Leif gestures for me to step in, and he follows, pressing the button for the fourth floor.

Maybe that's all it was to you.

Does Leif have feelings for me? Does he really think there's a difference between making love and fucking?

Because I don't know. I don't think anyone has ever made love to me. I was still a virgin when my mother kicked me out, and I had a few experiences during my time in Phoenix, but they were all quick fucks. Then on the island... That was rape, pure and simple.

What the hell is making love, anyway? I don't know what love is, so how could I know what *making* love is?

"Here we go." The elevator doors open and Leif gestures for me to go out.

"Okay." I walk to my apartment, pull out my key card, and slide it through.

"You okay for the time being?"

I turn to face him. "No. I won't be until you tell me what that text said."

"Damn it all to hell, Kelly." His mouth comes down on mine in a fiery kiss.

2

LEIF

I pry her lips open with my tongue.

How could she feel nothing? How can she think what we did was just a fuck?

I love this woman. God knows why, but I do. The heart wants what the heart wants. But I'm supposed to be protecting her, and if I let my heart get involved I may not think clearly. Plus, she's not ready for anything more than sex, if she's even ready for that. I break the kiss abruptly.

I wipe my mouth with the back of my hand. "Sorry about that."

"Are you?"

"I am," I say truthfully. "Because I think whatever this is between us has to stop."

She looks at the floor.

"Wouldn't you agree?" I ask.

"Yes, of course," she says, still gazing at her feet.

I tip her chin up so she's forced to look into my eyes. "Say it now. Say it to my face. Look into my eyes, Kelly, and tell me."

She looks away for a moment, but I cup both her cheeks and hold her face in place so her gaze can't waiver.

Even then, she attempts to look down.

"Damn it, Kelly. Look at me."

She obeys.

She obeys almost too quickly, as if it were instinctual.

"Answer me. You *will* fucking answer me."

"Yes," she grits out. "I think this should end."

"Very well." I grab my phone, trying to ease the ache in my heart. I pull up the text. I don't want to show it to her. It will scare her. It may send her into a tailspin.

But the text was meant for her. She's an adult, and it was not my place to hide it from her.

I glance at the words. I won't be leaving her tonight. I'll be staying on her couch. In fact, she won't be out of my sight until we put an end to this. The threat is so much worse than Brindley. So much worse than her mother, Racine.

We haven't even begun to figure this out.

I swallow, stand my ground.

And then I show her the text.

Her jaw drops, and the rosiness of her cheeks drains from her face.

"You see why I didn't want you to see it."

She gulps and hands the phone back to me, and I read the horrifying words once more.

I have a knife and a penis, and one of them is going inside you tonight.

3

KELLY

Not Brindley.
  Not any of the women.
    It's a man.
And I know who it is.

Except I don't. The man who used those exact words on the island always wore a mask.

His knife never went into me. I was obedient on the island. I didn't fight back as much as I probably should have. Macy says it's because of two things. One, after living with my mother, I was used to being obedient to avoid getting punished, and two, a dark part of me actually wanted the attention. When all the attention you know is negative, you begin to take it any way you can get it.

The man who said those words was called Mr. Smith.

A lot of them were called Mr. Smith.

But I called *this* Mr. Smith The Dark One because his hair was black as night, and so were his eyes. His skin was lightly tanned.

And he was the one...

I wasn't his favorite. He didn't always choose me. And when he didn't...I felt jealous.

"Did he have a favorite?" Macy asked me once.

"I don't know. Some of the men did."

"But did this one?"

"Like I said, I don't know. He chose me a lot. But sometimes he didn't."

"Perhaps you *were* his favorite."

The conversation jolted me at the time as I realized its truth. I *was* The Dark One's favorite, but he didn't exclusively choose me. That made me angry. Jealous.

Because though The Dark One did hunt me, did rape me, did utter those horrific words to me...

He never touched me with a knife. Once he caught me, all he did was fuck me. He didn't beat me, bruise me, or leave a scar on me.

And after a while, I no longer heard the threatening words.

Clearly he didn't mean them. Not about the knife anyway. His penis always went inside me, and though I didn't consent, he wasn't huge so it didn't hurt that much.

I began to covet The Dark One.

My work at the retreat center and with Macy made me realize exactly why. I never had any feelings for him. In fact, through therapy, I grew to resent his power over me. But during the time on the island, the jealousy grew from complex emotions from my childhood and even from my adulthood. No one protected me from the monsters under my bed, and when The Dark One chose someone else, the jealousy I felt was a manifestation of guilt. Guilt that someone else was being harmed instead of me. Because of my messed up childhood and my mother's abuse, my emotions were limited. I never experienced guilt in my life, so I didn't know what it was.

So I coveted The Dark One.

But now?

Now that I no longer covet him?

He appears to be back.

"I won't be leaving your side," Leif says.

I gulp again and nod.

"Do you have any idea who could have sent this?"

I nod again.

He cups my cheeks, gazes into my eyes. "Who, Kelly? Who? Because I swear to God, I'll fucking kill him."

My throat is constricted, and I'm not sure my voice will work.

"Who?" Leif says again, this time more gently.

"I think...one of the men from the island."

"Most of them are in prison," he says. "Except for the ones who disappeared."

"They disappeared?" I eke out.

"Yes, unfortunately, some of them did. Those who had enough money to buy a new identity, a new life."

"Apparently one of them is still around."

"Who was it, Kelly?"

I attempt to swallow the perpetual lump in my throat. "He was called Mr. Smith. All I can tell you is that he had very dark hair and dark eyes, a light tan."

Leif sighs. "That could be anyone."

"How can we make this stop? Whoever it is knows my phone number."

"We'll change your number."

I shake my head, sniffling back tears. "We already did that, and still he found me."

Leif opens the door for me, and we walk into my apartment.

"I'll sleep on the couch," he says.

"You don't have to."

"But you just said—"

"That was before I knew what this text said."

He rubs his forehead and then his temples. "I can't, Kelly."

"Why not?" I raise an eyebrow. "You didn't have any problem doing it before."

"You're right." He drops his gaze to the floor. "I didn't. I was wrong to even let it happen. But even if I weren't breaching my ethics, I sure as hell don't want to be used."

"Oh, for God's sake, Leif, I'm not *using* you."

He looks back up, meeting my gaze. His blue eyes sear into mine.

"But you are. How can you not see it?"

"And how can you possibly see it that way? You're a man. I know what men want. I knew before the island, and after the island, I sure as hell know even more."

"You wait a minute." He grits his teeth. "You will not link me with those men. I'm nothing like any of them."

"I didn't mean it that way, and you know it. But you are a man, and men like sex."

"Yeah. I am a man. And yeah, I do like sex. But I *can* control myself, Kelly, and I don't want to be used."

I scoff. "You seriously think I'm using you for sex?"

"I think it's pretty obvious. Two minutes ago you agreed

that we should stop sleeping together. And now this frightening text comes through, and you want me."

"Uh...I want you to stay in bed with me. Not on the couch. Did I say I wanted to have sex?"

"Oh my God..." He paces toward the kitchen.

"It's your job to protect me, isn't it? You mention it at every turn."

He turns, walks back toward me. "You and I both know what will happen if I get into bed with you. We'll fuck. That's called using a person. I wouldn't do it to you, and I'd appreciate if you wouldn't do it to me."

"You've already done it to me, Leif. That's what sex *is* for men."

He mutters something unintelligible. Then, "I'll sleep on the couch tonight."

I huff. "Suit your fucking self."

I HAVE A KNIFE AND A PENIS, and one of them is going inside you tonight.

The Dark One's eyes are narrowed, almost into slits.

He wears running shorts, running shoes, a white T-shirt, and a white mask that covers most of his face.

I'm wearing a flowing sundress but nothing else. Not even anything for my feet.

But I've been here a while, and my feet have become calloused. Only the sharpest stone hurts me now.

"Run..." he says, brandishing his silver knife.

I gape at the blade. It's at least six inches long.

When he says inside me, does he mean...

Truly inside *me*? Or does he just mean he's going to stab me?

Because it will happen, eventually. He's bigger, stronger, faster than I am.

Even so... I run...

I run hard and fast, my heart racing, my breath panting.

He gives me a head start. Most of them do. They like to work hard for their prey. It's part of the thrill of the hunt.

I've been here a while, so I know a lot of hiding places. Still, I run until I can no longer take another step, and even then I take three more.

Even though I never played volleyball for my high school team, which was always my dream, I tried to keep myself in shape. But nothing prepared me for going past my limitations like this place.

I don't stop running.

Eventually my body gives out, and I drop.

I dart my gaze around the forest. Where is the closest hiding place?

Doesn't matter, though, because here he comes.

The Dark One.

And he's—

He's wielding the glistening knife.

"Please..." *I say, my voice soft and raspy, out of breath.*

"Please what?"

"Please... Don't hurt me..."

Through my heavy-lidded eyes, I see him remove his tank top, his running shorts. He keeps his shoes and socks on.

He wears no underwear, and his dick springs out.

How can he have a hard-on after running so hard?

That's my last thought as he descends on me and I brace myself for the searing pain of the blade.

4

LEIF

My wrists are chafed and raw from being strung up. They've left no slack. Everything is adjusted to my height so if I stand, I'm fine.

But no one can stand for forty-eight hours.

The room is hot, and I'm in a constant sweat. The walls are gray concrete, but they're far from soundproof.

Wolf and Buck are somewhere near. I stopped wondering a while ago, and I'm even close to not caring.

I wince, and I can't help myself. I cry out at the pain in my wrist.

Then a scream from the room next to mine.

Not a shrill scream, but a manly scream.

I recognize the low voice. It belongs to Wolf.

"Stop it! No!"

Then another scream. This one curdles my blood.

Something is happening to Wolf.

Something harsh and painful.

And though I don't want to admit it, I know what they're doing to him.

But the knowledge does one thing for me. It gives me the strength to straighten my legs once more. I close my ears to Wolf's screams. As much as I can, anyway.

I close my eyes, focus. Focus like they taught us in training.

Focus on my mission and nothing else.

I will get out of here.

The Phoenix always fucking rises from the ashes.

But Wolf's screams...

They permeate my defenses...

Stop it! No! No! No...

Screams... More screams... More screams... Until —

"Please... Don't hurt me..."

The voice is not Wolf's.

It's feminine. Is there a woman here? Is there—

I JERK FORWARD, my eyes open.

I'm not back in Afghanistan, being held captive by insurgents.

I'm here. In New York. In Kelly's apartment. On Kelly's couch.

The screams...

They're not coming from Wolf in the next cell.

They're coming from Kelly.

I burst into action, rising, wearing only my underwear, and race into Kelly's room.

She's in bed, talking in her sleep. Screaming in her sleep.

I go to her, sit down, grip her shoulders. "Kelly! Kelly, wake up!"

"No, please don't hurt me! The knife, please!"

"Kelly, listen!" I shake her slightly more harshly. "It's just a nightmare. Wake up!"

Her eyes pop open.

"Where am I?"

"You're here, Kelly. Here in your apartment. It's me, Leif."

She jerks upward in bed, turns into my arms.

"Okay." I rub her soft hair. "It was just a nightmare, baby. It's okay."

The endearment slipped out, but I don't want to take it back.

She chokes back a sob.

She always does that. She's so strong. She refuses to cry.

Maybe she needs permission.

So I give it to her.

"It's okay, Kelly. It's okay to cry."

And then the sobs erupt.

She cries into my shoulder, and soon I'm wet with her tears. I ache to simply hold her, to kiss her chastely, tell her everything will be all right.

To confess to her how much I love her, how much I will protect her—always protect her. She has nothing to fear as long as I am with her.

But she doesn't want love from me. She made that clear.

So I can at least give her comfort.

She cries for five minutes, and then ten.

Until she finally sniffles, pulls away.

I glance around the room for some tissues. I don't see any.

"I'll be right back. I want to find you a Kleenex."

"No. Don't leave me." She grabs onto my arm.

"I'll be right here. I'm just going to your bathroom to get a tissue, and I'll return."

She nods, and I rise, find the tissues in her bathroom, and return with them. I pull one out and hand it to her.

She blows her nose more daintily than I expect.

"What can I get for you? Water? Herb tea?" I glance out the bedroom door toward the kitchen.

She blows her nose again. "Nothing."

"You sure?"

"Just stay here. Stay here with me. Please."

I'm not made of steel. Sleeping in bed next to the woman I love without touching her will be far from easy.

But I will do it.

And not just because it's my job.

My job description doesn't entail sleeping in the same bed with her.

I'll do it because I love her. Because I'll do anything in the world for her. Including sleeping with her but not *sleeping* with her, if that's what she needs. I should have done it in the first place.

"All right."

I let go of her and she lies down. I pull the covers over her. Then I go around the other side of the bed and climb in.

The cotton sheets are cool, not warm from her body because she's been sleeping on the other side.

I can't cuddle up to her to warm myself, but that's okay.

This is what she needs.

And I'm the one who doesn't want to be used.

I know all too well how nightmares can shake your soul. I learned to deal with them long ago. They come with the territory of being a SEAL. They will probably always be part of my life. They will always dredge up memories that I would choose to forget if I could.

Thinking about Wolf...

One of the four of us who didn't make it home.

There was Ghost—a ginger with the fairest skin ever. A young kid who died in a foxhole with Buck.

Wolf, called Wolf because his last name was Woolf, who died in captivity while Buck and I survived. God, the guilt I felt for that. Still feel.

Eagle, who—seriously—enjoyed bird watching, was killed by friendly fire. Still pisses me off.

Ace—so called because he had the best luck at poker I'd ever seen. He took his own life after the woman he had fallen in love with was killed by her older brother...for falling in love with an American.

That one hurt, mostly because I've never understood why he did it.

But I'm in love now. In love with the woman lying next to me.

Would I end my own life if hers ended?

No, I don't believe I would, but I sure wouldn't feel like going on.

And this is a woman who I just met, a woman who doesn't even return my feelings.

I remember when Buck's love, Amira, was killed by a suicide bomber. How I worried that Buck would go Ace's route, choose not to live anymore.

But he didn't.

Not the sprightly Buck.

Thank God, because he and Aspen are so perfect together.

Kelly's back is to me, and she sniffles into her pillow, shuddering slightly.

I ache to hold her, to comfort her, and yes, to warm myself with her body.

Would she ask me if she needed to be held? Do I have the strength to hold her and comfort her without shoving my dick inside her?

Yes, of course I do.

"Kelly?"

"What?" She sniffles again.

"Can I hold you?"

She doesn't turn. "Yes," she says into her pillow. "Please."

I scoot toward her, spoon her, take her warmth against my cold chest.

I expect her to complain about my cold skin, but she doesn't.

My cock reacts, of course. How can it not? I'm in love with her, and even if I weren't, she's so damned beautiful. So damned sexy.

I scoot back a bit so my erection won't bother her.

But she echoes my movements, scooting backward, wiggling her ass against my hard cock.

God, I know she's only using me. I want her so much. I love her so much.

She's wearing a T-shirt and bikini underwear. I could easily dissolve those in an instant.

As much as I want to slide my cock inside her, I can't help but remember the text.

I have a knife and a penis, and one of them is going inside you tonight.

I don't think a cock is what she needs tonight, whether or not she's aware of it.

Still, she wiggles her ass against me, and my cock aches. It fucking aches.

So I decide.

If she asks for sex, I'll give it to her. But she's going to have to ask for it. I may not be able to control how hard my cock gets, but I can certainly control what I do with it.

"Leif…"

"Yes?"

God, my cock is throbbing.

"Would you—"

A pounding echoes through the room.

Kelly jerks away from me, sitting upright. "Someone's at the door. Who would be at the door at this time of night?"

I sit up next to her, grip her shoulders. "You're safe with me."

"It's him." She trembles. "The text said tonight. Either the knife or his…would be inside me tonight."

I move away from her, rise, and pad out into the living room.

The pounding again. The pounding at the door. The pounding in my head.

I walk to the door, gaze out the peephole.

But no one's there.

Still wearing only my underwear, I rip the door open. "Where the fuck are you? Come out, you coward!"

I leave the apartment, making sure to close the door securely, and then I race down the hallway both ways, check the stairwell.

Damn. He must've had the elevator open and waiting.

I walk back to Kelly's apartment.

And then I see it. An envelope on the floor right outside her door.

I pick it up.

Not much frightens me anymore, but I'm sure apprehensive about looking inside this envelope.

I close the door to Kelly's apartment and lock it. I place the envelope on the table. Before anything else, I need to make sure Kelly's okay.

I walk back to her bedroom. She's still sitting up in bed, her eyes wide.

"Who was it?"

"No one. I checked the hallways and the stairwell. Whoever it was must've had an elevator waiting."

"Who could have gotten in here? Through all the security?"

"I don't know," I say. "But I'm damned well going to find out."

"No!" she nearly shrieks. "Don't leave me. Please. It's the middle of the night."

"Sweetheart, you'll be perfectly safe."

"Please don't."

"I'll get Buck—" I shake my hand. "Shit. Buck and Aspen went to Colorado for a few days."

"There's no one else?"

"I'll get a security guard from downstairs."

She jumps to her feet. "What good are they? Whoever pounded on my door already got past them."

She's right, of course.

"What if we call Brindley? Ask her to come down."

"She smaller than I am. She can't protect me."

"But at least you won't be alone, Kelly. One of us is going

to have to go downstairs and figure out what happened with security. I certainly don't expect that to be you."

In fact, I need to go back to my apartment next door and grab a second gun. I should have had both pieces on me tonight after that text message came through.

Kelly races around the room frantically. "I'm getting dressed. I'm going with you."

"Kelly, no—"

"Shut up, Leif. Just shut up. I'm not going to stay here alone or with Brindley or with anyone else other than you. If *you* go, Leif, I'm going."

"Kelly…"

"This isn't up for argument. I'm coming along." She runs into the bathroom and returns with her hair brushed and pulled into a ponytail. She scrambles into a pair of jeans, moccasin slippers, and a pink sweatshirt.

"I'm ready."

I'm dressed as well, and I wish I could talk her out of this, but already I know that would be futile. An ultimate exercise in futility.

"Kelly, this isn't a joke."

She sets her hands on her hips. "Do I look like I'm joking?"

Kelly never looks like she's joking, but that's beside the point. At least if she's with me, I can shield her with my body. Do my best to keep her safe.

"All right. First we're going back over to my place. I need to get my piece."

"You mean you're not armed?"

"No. I wasn't expecting any trouble tonight."

"After that fucking text? You weren't expecting any trouble?" She swats me on the shoulder. Not enough to hurt, but not lightly either.

"Do you want to stand here and argue with me, or do you want to go next door so I can get my other pistol? Then we'll figure out what's going on."

"Fine," she huffs.

I take her hand, and I'm surprised when she doesn't pull away. When she's in this kind of a mood, she normally doesn't like to be touched. But her fear is overpowering her spitefulness. We walk the few steps to my apartment and I open the door.

I allow her to go in before me. Quick as a flash, I move to the safe I keep my weapons in, grab my other Glock, and shove it in the back of my jeans. No time to mess with the shoulder holster. My ankle holster is already in place.

"Kelly," I say seriously, "why don't you stay here in my place? I know it's safe. I'll lock you in. Nothing can happen to you here. No one's expecting you to be here."

She bites her lower lip. Good, she's thinking about it.

"I want to go with you."

"I don't have a lot of time to argue," I say.

"Then don't."

"My place is secure. Please. Stay here. If anything happened to you..."

I shake my head. If anything happened to Kelly, the woman I love, I'd get a good dose of what Ace went through.

She swallows. Not audibly, but I see her throat move. She's thinking about it again. Good.

"Please, Kelly." I cup her cheek, her skin so silky.

"All right, Leif. But damn it, you'd better come back to me."

5

KELLY

A look of pure relief crosses Leif's face. He truly is concerned. But of course he is. It's his job.

He stares at me, and for a moment I think he's going to kiss me, but he doesn't.

"I'll be back as soon as I can. You have your phone on you?"

"Crap. I left it at my place."

"All right. There's a landline here. The phone is in the bedroom, it's a secure line. Stay in the bedroom, and if the phone rings twice and then stops, it's me. Answer the next time. But if it rings more than twice without stopping, don't answer."

I nod, fear pulsing through me.

"Everything will be all right, Kelly. I'll probably be back very soon. But if I'm not, you will get a call. So listen for it."

"All right." I try to calm my beating heart. "Leif?"

"Yes?"

"Please. Please come back." I tear up, but damn it, I can't cry. Not again.

"The Phoenix always rises." He drops something onto the table by the door. "You stay here. No matter what." He closes the door behind him.

I hear all the locks click.

But still... I don't feel secure.

I only feel secure when Leif is with me.

What exactly am I feeling for him? I don't know what happiness feels like. I don't know what love feels like. I have no point of reference.

And at the moment, fear for my life is kind of overriding everything else.

The Dark One must be behind this. Who else would use that exact phrase?

I have a knife and a penis, and one of them is going inside you tonight.

I shudder.

Funny. All those times The Dark One chose me on the island, he said the same words. He never put the knife inside me, and I grew less fearful each time. I grew more jealous when he chose someone other than me.

I was still apprehensive, of course, but I no longer feared him on the island.

But damn... I fear him now. Somehow he's come back. He's found me, and I don't know how I'll escape. If he could get past security, get to the fourth floor to pound on my door...

Then he can get anywhere.

I'll never be safe from him.

"LINE UP, GIRLS," Diamond says. "Mr. Smith will make his choice."

When we're put on display for the men, we're naked. Sometimes we're allowed to wear clothes during the hunt because the men enjoy ripping them off us. But while they're making their choice, we have to be naked. Completely on display. Like window dressing.

The Dark One has chosen me the last three times. He will choose me again this evening. He seems to like me.

Still, I'm apprehensive. It's better not to be chosen. It's better to be safe in the dorm.

The Dark One is dressed in a suit and tie. Most of the men are when they make their selection. Most of them also wear a mask, and The Dark One is no exception. He wears his white mask that covers most of his face. Only his dark hair and dark eyes are visible.

He walks by slowly, looking each of us up and down lasciviously. When he comes to me, he smiles.

"Hello, Opal."

"Good day, sir."

We're instructed to call them all sir.

"You're looking lovely, as usual."

"Thank you, sir."

He continues, scanning Tiger Eye next to me, and then Crystal and Lapis.

When he reaches the end of the line, he returns, again walking slowly, looking each of us over.

Until he stops in front of me.

He gazes into my eyes.

I swallow, knowing I'm about to be chosen.

He holds out his hand, and I tremble.

But he takes Tiger Eye's hand. "You're my choice," he says.

A soft gasp escapes my throat.

He didn't choose me? What's wrong with me?

Tiger Eye is beautiful, with her medium dark skin, brown hair and eyes. But all the women here are beautiful.

I'll have the day off. It's too late now for any other men to come and make a choice. I should be ecstatic, as all the other girls clearly are.

As soon as Mr. Smith leaves, Crystal and Jade heave heavy sighs of relief.

Diamond returns. "All right, girls. Congratulations. Enjoy your time off."

And I want to. I truly do.

But all I feel is the dead weight of jealousy burning in my gut.

What's wrong with me? Why didn't he choose me?

"Thank God," Amethyst says, once Diamond is out of earshot. "I'm going to my room."

"I'm going to the main room to watch TV," Moonstone says.

"I'll join you." From Onyx.

"Opal?" Garnet says. "Do you want to come?"

I don't reply. My hands are curled into fists, my knuckles white.

"Opal?" Garnet says again.

"He should've chosen me," I say under my breath.

Garnet's eyes go wide.

Then she heads to her room. Once she's dressed, she'll go watch old sitcoms. Moonstone, Onyx, and Garnet always watch those stupid shows.

And I'll go to my room, eat my evening meal when it comes, and wonder what made me so unchoosable.

6

LEIF

I hate leaving Kelly alone, but she's safer locked in my place than she'll be coming with me into something unknown.

I choose not to take the elevator down and instead head toward the stairwell. Gun in hand, I look each way and behind me as I slink down the stairs sideways. When I get to the main floor, I open the door as quietly as I can, still holding my gun, still staying hyperaware of my surroundings.

The lobby is well lit, and I head toward the—

I gasp as I race to the security desk. The security guard on duty is asleep, his head slumped over the table.

There's no doorman at the building because you can't enter without a key card.

Usually at least three guards are on duty every night, but I only see one. One with his head slumped over the desk.

I shake him. "Hey, wake up!" I place two fingers on his neck. Thank God. He has a pulse.

He's out cold though. I pull his head up and check his neck.

Sure enough, a red mark. He was injected with something. Whatever it is made him pass out, and he isn't waking up anytime soon.

Where the hell are the other two guards?

I call Reid quickly.

"Leif? What is it?"

"I'm calling 911 after I get off the phone with you. Someone got into the building tonight. Pounded on Kelly's door. I tried to chase him down the hall but he was already gone. I'm in the lobby now, at security. The guy at the desk is out cold. The other two are nowhere to be found."

"Damn. I'm on my way."

I call 911, explain the situation, and wait for the police to arrive.

They'll dust for fingerprints, but already I know they won't find anything. Whoever did this knows well how to cover his tracks. I know because I know how to cover *my* tracks.

This is the work of a professional.

No one other than a professional could get into this building.

I case the place, checking all the restrooms, everywhere on the first floor. Once the police get here, they'll check the other floors. Then it dawns on me. "My God. The other women!"

Two other women live on the fourth floor, and Brindley lives on the fifth. Aspen and Buck are gone, so I don't need to worry about them.

Man, I wish Buck were here. He and I could cover the building in half the time.

Reid arrives before the police. I'm not surprised. He's wearing jeans, moccasins, and a hooded sweatshirt.

"Leif! Did you find anything?"

"Main floor's clean. Now that you're here, I need to go check on the girls on the fourth and fifth floor. Kelly's locked in my apartment."

"Good. I'll stay here and wait for the police."

I nod and head up the staircase. I head to the fourth floor first. How am I supposed to do this? If I pound on Marianne's and Francine's doors, they'll freak out.

I decide to call instead.

Once I've spoken to both of them and told them to make sure their doors are locked and stay in their apartment until they hear further, I head to my own place.

I knock softly. "Kelly?"

No response. She probably can't hear me as I told her to stay in my bedroom.

So I make the call. Two rings, and then I hang up. I wait thirty seconds and call again.

"Leif?" she says breathlessly.

"Yeah, baby, it's me. I'm right outside the door."

"I'm coming."

"No. You stay locked in. I'm checking out this floor. Marianne and Francine are safely locked in their apartments. I'm going to go up and check on Brindley."

"Did you find him? You have to tell me what's going on, Leif."

"I don't know anything yet. But you're safe. That's the most important thing. I'll check in again as soon as I can."

"Leif, please—"

"I have to go, Kelly. I'm sorry." I end the call.

And damn, it about kills me. Hanging up on the woman I love.

I head back to the stairwell and walk to the fifth floor, still with stealth. Once I reach the door of Brindley's apartment, I call her.

Both Francine and Marianne picked up quickly, as did Kelly after I let the phone ring twice.

Come on Brindley. Answer your damned phone.

The phone finally clicks to voicemail.

Hi, this is Brindley. I'm so sorry I missed your call. Please leave a message and I'll get back to you right away.

"Brindley, it's Leif Ramsey. I need you to pick up the phone. Please. I'm going to keep calling."

I try again and again, but it goes to voicemail each time.

I could pound on the door, but in the middle of the night that will scare her.

But I have no other choice.

I throw my fist at the door, pounding as hard as I can. "Brindley!"

Nothing. My God, she must be a sound sleeper.

"Brindley! It's Leif! Please come to the door!"

Nothing.

And damn... I don't have a good feeling about it.

At least Kelly is safe.

Unfortunately, I don't have a key card for Brindley's apartment. Only for Kelly's, since I was hired specifically to watch over her.

But Reid is downstairs. He has keys to each one.

The fourth floor is secure, and I checked the rest of the fifth floor, and it's secure as well.

I lock the doors to the stairwells at the fourth and fifth

floors so no one except Reid and me can get in. Then, on my way down, I check the third, second, and first floors. All clear, and I lock them up.

I return to the main floor, where I find Reid talking to two uniformed police officers and several EMTs getting the security guard onto a stretcher.

"Good." Reid motions to me. "Here's one of my security team. He can tell you more."

"Sir," one of the uniformed officers says to me.

"It's Leif. Leif Ramsey. I'm the one who found the guard passed out."

"And the other two?"

"It's a mystery," I say. "They weren't here when I came down."

"All right," the other blue says. "Start at the beginning, Mr. Ramsey."

I run through the events for them, starting with the pounding on Kelly's door, all the while thinking about Brindley. I've got to get Reid's key.

"Did you see anything suspicious at all?" the first officer asks.

"Only that two guards were missing, and one was out cold. Whoever did this knows how to cover their tracks."

"We'll get forensics in here. No one can cover their tracks that well."

I simply nod.

This is a uniformed officer, not a detective. I hate to burst his bubble, but forensics isn't going to find anything.

"There's something else," I say specifically to Reid. "I checked with the other two women who live on the fourth floor, and they're both secure and safe and locked in. But the girl on the fifth floor, Brindley McGregor, didn't answer her phone, and she didn't come to the door when I pounded and yelled."

Reid's eyes widen. "Oh my God."

"I know. I don't have a key to her place."

Reid pulls out his pocket wallet, grabs a key card. "This is the master. It'll get you in. Take one of the officers with you."

I nod. The cop—his name tag says Powers—heads to the stairwell with me. Both of us draw our guns.

Officer Powers is huffing and puffing by the time we walk up five floors. Aren't police officers supposed to be in good shape?

I unlock the stairwell door, and then I lead the way to Brindley's apartment.

"Did you check out all the other empty apartments up here?"

"I didn't have that much time," I say, "but I did check the doors. They're all locked."

"We're going to need to check all these empty apartments."

"I agree. I would've done it, but I didn't have the time."

Officer Powers lets out a soft scoff. Fine. I'm used to law enforcement thinking they know more than I do. In some cases, they do. Powers though? Not a chance.

We reach Brindley's door, and I try calling her. Again, no answer.

I pound on the door again. "Brindley! It's Leif! Open up!"

Once more, no response.

Officer Powers pounds on the door. "It's the police, ma'am. Please open the door!"

"I think we have to go in," I say.

"Yep."

I slide the master key through the reader and open the door. "Brindley!"

I head straight to her bedroom.

The door is closed.

I knock. "Brindley! Open up! It's Leif Ramsey!"

"You're going to scare her," Powers says.

"She didn't hear the phone. She didn't hear the pounding on the outside door. What do you suggest I do?"

"Open the door."

"That's what I'll do next, if she doesn't answer."

Officer Powers pushes me out of the way. "Christ," he murmurs. Then he opens the door.

He walks in a few steps, and—

Thud.

It reverberates out into the hallway where I'm standing.

I rush into Brindley's room—

And I gasp.

7

KELLY

A birthday card sits on the table at breakfast. I'm eighteen today, halfway through my senior year of high school.

The envelope is pink. I'm not a huge fan of the color, but it seems to connote gentleness. I haven't known a lot of gentleness in my life.

I recognize my mother's handwriting on the outside of the card. It says simply Kelly.

"Mom?" I yell.

She doesn't reply, which doesn't necessarily mean she's not here. Mom doesn't always reply when she is here. A lot of times she likes to pretend I don't exist.

It's been that way since I grew as strong as she is. She can no longer smack me around and throw me in the closet, so we pretty much just coexist. At least I usually get enough to eat these days. I can earn my own money babysitting, and though I don't have a lot of friends, I occasionally get invited somewhere for dinner.

Sometimes Mom is home, and sometimes she's not.

She doesn't tell me where she goes or where she's been, yet I'm *supposed to always relay my whereabouts to her. Which I do. Call it habit. Today I'm eighteen. A legal adult. Perhaps I no longer must do as she says.*

I scoff. What a nice thought. Except I still live here, in a house she rents.

I pick up the card, look at my name.

The envelope is perfect and pink. I turn it over, slide my thumb beneath the—

"Ouch!"

I suck my thumb into my mouth.

Freaking paper cut.

I let out a sarcastic chuckle.

Nice foreshadowing. Nothing from my mother is ever good.

Eight years ago, she gave me my own deflated volleyball for my birthday after locking me in the closet. Then she demanded that I thank her for such a thoughtful gift.

Today's thoughtful gift begins with a paper cut.

I finish unsealing the envelope and pull out the card.

The card itself is also pink, with sprays of flowers and different pastel colors. In script it says, For my daughter on her birthday.

Yes, most others who receive this card will open it and find a loving message.

I haven't received any words of love from my mother in about five years. It all coincided with the point when she could no longer lock me in the closet.

At least back then, I got words of love on occasion. The next moment she would be vicious, but for those few seconds, I felt...

What did I feel exactly?

Not loved, for sure. I don't have a clue what that feels like. I have some friends, and I've had a boyfriend or two. I enjoy being with them, but do I love them?

Hell if I know.

I open the card.

I force myself to read the message before I head straight to my mother's writing at the bottom.

A daughter like you is a rare gem. I'm thankful every day for you, sweetheart. Happy eighteenth birthday.

Then my mother's handwriting.

You're an adult now. I expect you to be out of the house by the end of the day.

I gasp.

Seriously? She's kicking me out in the middle of my senior year of high school?

My God, this is vicious, even for her.

Where am I supposed to go? I don't have a job. She never let me have one. I was supposed to be here so I could fix her meals and clean her house and do whatever the hell else she wanted me to do.

Fine.

I just won't leave.

What's she going to do?

I find out the next day.

She has me arrested for trespassing and escorted off the premises by a police officer.

So I'm alone.

But I'm not locked in a closet. That must count for something.

TWO HOURS HAVE PASSED, and I can't sleep.

What am I going to do? I need sleep. I'm supposed to work tonight. My shift doesn't start until four, but still...

Leif, where are you?

I both like and dislike that I want him here.

I've never relied on another person since I graduated from high school and got the job at the diner. So why am I relying on Leif?

Sex doesn't mean anything. I've been around the block—if you call sporadic experiences and then five years on the fucking island the block—enough to know that.

I need to stop counting on Leif. I never wanted full-time protection in the first place. I know better than to rely on anyone else. In fact, since my mother often let me starve when I was younger, I've relied on no one but myself for pretty much my entire life.

I close my eyes, squeeze them shut. That only makes me more tense.

So I open my eyes. You can't force sleep, after all. Despite all the crap in my life, I never had trouble sleeping. Sleep was an escape, and I relished it.

But tonight? Tonight I can't sleep. Leif. Images of Leif in trouble whirl through my mind.

What the hell is this? This thing I'm feeling? Why can't I just—

And it dawns on me.

It's an emotion I've never felt before. One I couldn't even name.

Worry. Concern.

It's kind of like fear, but different. I'm focused on someone other than myself.

I'm worried about Leif.

Worried for his safety. Because I want him to return. I want him with me.

I'm worried about him.

And my God... I hate the feeling.

Perhaps it's better to live the way I did before, knowing only two emotions. Anger and fear.

Because if this is emotion, I sure as hell don't like it.

I sigh and sit up in bed. I promised Leif I wouldn't leave the bedroom, but I'm hungry. Strange, given that I also feel nauseous. Nothing about how I feel right now makes any sense.

I just want a snack. A little snack, but I can't break my promise to Leif.

I sit in bed, twiddling my thumbs. Maybe I could try to read.

I scan the small bookshelf next to his TV.

Nothing strikes my fancy. Not that I thought it would.

The problem is the hunger. Hunger while I'm nauseated. Makes no sense, but it's there, and the fact that I can't sate it makes it weigh even heavier on my mind.

It's the worry for Leif that's making me feel sick. Like there's a cannonball lodged in my gut. That if he doesn't come back to me safely, I may not be able to go on.

"Fuck it," I say out loud. I get out of bed. I'm still in my jeans and pink sweatshirt—God, I hate pink. Why do I even have this thing?—and I open my door slowly and head to the kitchen.

Just a snack, and then I'll go back to bed. I pour myself a glass of water and open the refrigerator. A slice of cheese. That sounds good. I grab the package of cheddar slices, peel one off, and take a bite.

I swallow, and it lands like a brick in the pit of my stomach.

Yuck. I throw the rest of it in the trash, and then I take my water and head back to the bedroom. First though, I take a quick walk around the rest of the apartment. I know Leif checked it all out, but I just want to be sure.

Something's off.

Something doesn't belong here.

And then I zero in on it.

There's a white envelope sitting on the table by the door.

8

LEIF

Blood.

So much blood.

I'm no stranger to blood.

But Brindley...

So young...

Already such a hard life, growing up in the system, and then being captured and sent to that horrific island...

And now...

My bowels clench.

I've seen death.

I've *caused* death.

But it never gets any fucking easier.

Officer Powers is on the floor, passed out cold. Apparently he's never seen death. Every officer does at some point. He'll never forget this moment once he comes to.

I look at Brindley's lifeless body.

Blood seeps through the comforter.

Yet her face is serene.

Yellowish pale in death, but still serene.

I remove the cover, and then I nearly lose the contents of my stomach.

The source of the blood...

Between her legs.

I have a knife and a penis, and one of them is going inside you tonight.

God...

Oh my God.

Even though I know she's dead, I instinctively touch my fingers to her neck.

No pulse, but something surprises me.

Her neck is still warm.

Not full living-human warmth, but not the ice of death.

Whoever did this... Whoever did this is nearby.

Perhaps still in this apartment.

Self-preservation kicks in, and I step over Officer Powers's body, my gun drawn, to check the rest of the place.

It's clean, and I already checked the fifth floor earlier. But I didn't check inside Brindley's apartment. I did, however, lock the doors to the stairwell and disable the elevators. So it's possible whoever did this is still somewhere on the fifth floor. If he was still in Brindley's apartment when I did my first check, he could still be anywhere else on the fifth floor. Except...

Damn.

I was so anxious to get to Brindley, I didn't relock the door to the stairwell. If he was trapped on the fifth floor...he's most likely gone by now.

I didn't secure any of the top floors. Buck and Aspen are

the only ones who live higher than floor five, and they're not currently here.

So he's either somewhere on the top floors or he made it down. But he couldn't have. I locked the doors to all the other floors lower than five.

I return to Brindley's bedroom where Powers is finally coming to.

"You okay?" I ask him.

"Yeah. Sorry about that."

I feel for him, but maybe he'll leave his cowboy attitude at the door now.

I offer him a hand, but he shakes his head.

"I'm okay. But thanks."

He gets to his feet and then turns to regard Brindley's body in the bed.

"Damn," he says. "How old was she anyway?"

"I don't know. Early twenties."

"After all these girls have already been through."

"I know it."

"What happened to her?"

"Sure you want to know?"

"For God's sake." Powers pulls off the cover, and then lets out a gasp before passing out again with a bigger thud this time.

I take the opportunity to call Reid.

"Leif? What'd you find?"

"It's not good news."

"Nothing will surprise me at this point."

"You sure?"

"Just tell me what you found, damn it."

I clear my throat, nearing puking. "Brindley's gone, Reid. She's dead."

Silence.

"Reid?"

More silence. Then, "Fuck. How? How could any of this have happened? We worked so hard to protect these women. "

I'm not sure what to say. It's my job to protect the women as well. Especially Kelly, but all of them. Reid isn't the only one who failed here. We both did.

"This is going to kill Zee," he finally says.

But his voice says more. His voice says it's killing him too.

I swallow hard against the nausea. "And Kelly. Because I think..."

"What, damn it. What?"

I gulp down the acid in my throat. "I think this is a message. And I think it was meant for Kelly."

Another pause, and in my mind's eye I see the look of horror on Reid's face.

Finally, "What the hell are you talking about?"

"Kelly got another text. A really nasty one. What happened to Brindley..."

"Just tell me. I'm on my way up, if I can get through the cops guarding the stairwells. What the fuck happened to her?"

I flash then.

I flash to everything I saw during the worst times of my tours overseas.

And I realize I have to be blunt with Reid.

"Someone shoved a fucking knife up her cunt," I say. "Violated her in the worst way, and she bled to death."

WOLF'S SCREAMS PERMEATE ME.

We knew this was a possibility. That insurgents would do whatever it took to get information out of us.

But they don't know Navy SEALs.

We never talk.

We know what could happen, and we don't talk.

So I wait. Willing the strength to my legs to stand, to ease the pain in my wrists and arms and shoulders.

I stand tall, and I stand proud.

For I am tall and I am proud. I'm a fucking Navy SEAL.

And they will not break me.

Something treads across my feet. I look down.

Another rat scurries across.

Damn. Even rat meat would taste good right now. I'm starving, and I can't remember when someone last brought me water and held it to my lips.

Another rat scurries by, and I cock my head. Something seems different.

Then I realize what it is.

It's silence.

Wolf's screams have ceased.

Which means...

They stopped their torture, and they would only do that for two reasons.

Either Wolf talked...and I know he didn't...

Or they killed him.

They fucking killed him.

Have they gotten to Buck?

I haven't heard him, but he could be in another building for all

I know. I don't know how many people are in here. I knew Wolf is —was—next to me because I recognized his voice. I'm not sure how long we've even been here. Only a few days, and the only time they uncuff us is to give us the meager meals they provide.

Still...I am the Phoenix.

And I will rise.

9

KELLY

I tremble as I pick up the small white envelope. Nothing is written on the front of it, so maybe it doesn't belong to Leif. Normally I'd never open someone else's mail, but I'm bored, and I'm frightened, and I'm... Fuck it.

I slide my thumb under—

"Fuck!"

I suck the tip of my thumb, flashing back to the last time I got a paper cut opening an envelope.

My eighteenth birthday...

How many envelopes have I opened since then?

A few bills, some junk mail.

During those five years I was on my own, and the tiny bit of mail I've gotten since I've been here at this apartment.

All those times, I've managed to open the damned envelope without cutting myself.

A feeling of impending doom washes over me.

The last time I cut myself on an envelope, my mother abandoned me. I had no feelings for the woman, but I had nowhere else to go. If it weren't for a friend taking me in, I'd have ended up on the streets.

I breathe in deeply once, twice, three times. Try to settle my heart rate.

But it's no use.

I take my thumb out of my mouth. The bleeding has died down enough so that I can finish opening the envelope. More careful this time, I tear the paper and take out what's inside.

It's another sheet of paper, folded into thirds. A simple yellow sheet of paper with lines, from a legal pad.

I swallow, gathering my courage. It's probably nothing, right?

I unfold it slowly. It's handwritten in blue ink.

Hello Kelly.

My heart jerks. It's for me?

Yes, I know your real name, Opal. I found you. You know you were always my favorite. I know how you used to get jealous when I chose another girl over you. That's why I did it. To make you want me more. Then you were taken away from me, but I found you.

Did you see who I chose tonight? Does that make you want me more?

You were taken away from me, but I found you, and you will be mine. Because if you aren't?

What I did to your friend, I will do to you.

Mr. Smith

I freeze. The yellow sheet of paper flutters to the floor.

All those times on the island, The Dark One made that same threat with the knife, but he never acted on it. I mean, he did. He used his cock to violate me, but that was a hell of a lot better than a knife.

I considered myself lucky.

I considered myself lucky in many ways while on the island. I had a roof over my head, as much nutritious food as I wanted to keep me strong. The only time I was truly physically harmed—enough to be sent to the infirmary—was when a different man, known as Mr. Wilson, sliced into my thighs, giving me the scars that I bear.

So many women had it much worse than I did, and Aspen probably had it the worst.

I began to rely on The Dark One. In a warped way, I looked forward to his visits, and I was angry and jealous when he chose someone else. After all his threats, he never hurt me with the knife. He gave me the attention I craved— the attention I never had any other time in my life. So when he chose another? I got angry. Jealous.

Because those were the only emotions I knew at that time.

How did he know that? How did he read me so well?

God, I was fucked up.

And now...

Now he's back.

Leif. I need Leif. I don't have my cell phone. He told me not to leave his bedroom.

I scramble back into the bedroom, closing and locking the door.

My throat is parched, but I left my glass of water outside. Doesn't matter. I go to the bathroom, hold my head under the sink, take a drink from the faucet as best I can.

Doesn't help. My throat is still parched, sore, tight.

I'm frozen on the inside. Frozen in fear. I barely make it back to Leif's bed on my jelly legs, and I lie down, curling into a fetal position and pulling the covers over me.

The landline unit sits on the nightstand, glowing at me as if it's lit from within.

Leif. I need to call Leif.

He promised that the landline was secure, so I reach forward, my hands trembling, and pick up the receiver. I punch in his number.

"Hello?" A female voice.

"Who the hell is this?" I demand.

"Who the hell is *this*? You called me."

"I'm looking for Leif."

"I think you have the wrong number."

A tiny bit of relief swims through me. Of course. I punched in the wrong number. My fingers aren't working.

I try again, this time carefully looking at each key as I push it.

It rings.

Again.

Five rings, until—

"Kelly! What is it?"

"I..."

"Are you all right?"

"I need you."

"Are you hurt? What happened?"

"There was a letter. I opened it."

"What letter?"

"From..."

"Oh, fuck. I forgot about that. It was on the floor after... Anyway, I put it in my pocket and I left it on the table at my place."

"It's from him, Leif. The one who sent the text. He's not going to stop. He's coming after me, and he threatened..."

"Threatened what?" Leif's voice is low, angry.

"He said he was going to do to me what he did to my friend. I don't understand. I don't have any friends, unless you count the women here, and we're not really friends. I don't know what it meant, Leif."

Silence for a few seconds.

When I can't take it anymore— "Leif? Please."

"Oh, baby. I'll be right there."

The phone goes dead. I replace the receiver on the landline unit, crawl back under my covers.

I don't know how quickly Leif will get here. I have no idea where he is.

Until he bursts through the bedroom door. I gasp in fear, even though I recognize his face.

"Leif, thank God. I didn't know where you were."

"No one else can get in here, Kelly. This is my place, remember?"

"Thank God." I scramble out of bed and launch myself into his arms.

He kisses the top of my head.

"Did you read the letter?" I ask.

"No. Where is it?"

"I don't know. I—"

He kisses my head again. "It's probably where you left it. Somewhere near the table by the door."

"It's from him. One of the men from the island. The one who's texting me."

"Oh, baby..." He pulls away so that he can meet my gaze. "I swear to God, Kelly. No one will harm you. I will die first."

My eyes have adjusted to the darkness of the bedroom, and his eyes... Something in Leif's eyes...

He's serious. Completely serious.

This man will die before any harm comes to me.

He means it. He means those words. He means them as if he had his hand on the Bible swearing to them under oath.

I mean something to this man. And those feelings I've been having… Those feelings I can't put a name to…

No. It's not possible.

"Kelly, I need to look at the letter. Are you okay here in the bedroom?"

I shake my head vehemently. "I'm coming with you."

He nods, takes my hand, and leads me out of the bedroom toward the living room where the yellow paper still lies on the floor.

"Aren't you going to pick it up?" I ask.

"Not yet." He leads me to the kitchen area, where he opens the cupboard and pulls out a box marked *nitrile gloves*. He pulls out two blue disposable gloves and puts them on.

"What's that for?"

"I don't want to disturb any fingerprints that might be on the paper."

My heart sinks to my stomach. "Oh, Leif. I already touched it."

Leif draws in a breath, lets it out slowly. "All right, Kelly. You weren't thinking. You were scared."

"I don't know what's wrong with me. I know better than to mess with potential evidence."

"You had no idea who it was from."

"I shouldn't have even opened it. This is your apartment. I was out of line, and I'm sorry, Leif."

His gaze softens, and the searing blue of his eyes melts me.

"Baby, it's okay. No one's going to think anything of it."

"I hope not."

"I promise." He finishes snapping on the second glove. "Now let's look at that letter."

Still gripping his hand, I follow him. Leif kneels, picks up the letter, his eyes widening as he reads it.

He glances at a small spot on the paper. "There's a speck of blood on this letter. Maybe we could find some DNA."

"That's probably my blood." I hold up my thumb. "I got a paper cut when I was opening the envelope."

"I see. Now that I look at it, the color's not quite right. It's too fresh to have come from whoever wrote the letter."

"What can we do now?"

He folds the letter and then slowly turns to face me, his jaw clenched and his eyes unreadable. "Kelly, I have to tell you something."

My body goes numb once more. "What?"

"He refers to a friend in this letter."

"I know."

"Kelly, let's go sit down."

My legs crumple, and Leif steadies me as we walk to the couch. He sits down and pulls me into his lap.

Being so close to Leif, having him care for me, normally gives me so much comfort. Comfort I've never had in my life. This time, all I can feel is fear. Fear about what he's going to tell me.

"Baby, I need you to listen to me."

I nod. "All right."

"Brindley... She's *gone*, Kelly."

I furrow my brow. "Did she go home? That's odd. We just saw her earlier."

"No, Kelly. She didn't go home. Brindley is dead."

My heart stops. I can't move. Have I stopped living? I feel no heartbeat. I take no breath. I can't move. I can't speak. I can't unclench my hand around Leif's arm.

Brindley's my friend? The friend The Dark One referred to in the letter?

Brindley and I aren't friends. We were never friends. I'm not friends with any women from the island. I'm not friends with...anyone.

But of course The Dark One would mean a woman from the island.

Of course The Dark One—

Murdered. Brindley. Murdered. Is my heart beating? Am I alive? Or did The Dark One come for me?

Numbness.

My breath...

I don't know where I am or who I am or what I am.

I know only Leif.

"The letter..." The words come out of my mouth in a hushed whisper.

"Yes. Clearly he was referring to Brindley."

Then I can't speak. Again, I can't move. Am I still living? Is my heart still working?

I treated Brindley so badly, and now...

I'll never be able to make it up to her.

Worse than that... This is my fault. She's dead because of me.

"Baby..."

I don't reply.

"Kelly, baby, what can I do for you? What do you need?"

I open my mouth, willing my voice to work. "My fault."

"How can you say that?"

Tears well in my eyes. "It's always my fault, Leif. Everything. I was a bad girl. That's why I got locked in the closet."

His eyes widen. "Locked in the closet? Kelly, baby, what are you talking about?"

"I'll never be able to make it up to her."

"Make what up to whom?"

"Brindley. I treated her badly. Now... Because of me... Lock me in the closet, Leif."

"Kelly, I will never lock you in any closet."

"But it's what I deserve. Please."

He grips my shoulders, shakes me. "You get ahold of yourself right now, Kelly Taylor. You listen to me. None of this is your fault. And I will never lock you in any closet. No one will ever lock you in any closet as long as I live. Do you hear me?"

I don't reply.

He shakes me again. "Do you fucking hear me?"

10

LEIF

Her lips part, but she says nothing.

"Kelly, please..." I stop shaking her. I don't think it's helping.

Her eyes are glazed over, and tears well in the bottom of them. She seems to be focusing on something in the distance, but the only thing in the distance is the wall.

Someone in Kelly's past locked her in a closet. Most likely her bitch mother, Racine. I'm so full of rage right now I can hardly contain myself, but I need to stay calm for Kelly. But how the hell do I stay calm? I just learned more about the abuse endured by the woman I love during her childhood, and I just witnessed a horrific crime perpetrated on an innocent young girl.

How the fuck am I supposed to stay calm?

I rise, cradling Kelly in my arms like a child. I walk to my bedroom and put her back in bed.

I kiss her forehead. "Try to sleep, baby. You're safe here."

"Closet..." she murmurs.

I kiss her forehead again. "Never. No one will ever put you in the closet again."

"Bad girl..."

"No. You were never a bad girl, Kelly. And now you're a grown woman. A wonderful beautiful woman. A woman I love."

The words came out on their own, but I can't bring myself to regret them. She may not return my feelings, but I needed to say it.

Her eyes widen slightly, but I'm not sure she grasps what I just said. She seems to be reliving her past. She's exhausted and frightened, and I just told her that Brindley is dead.

She closes her eyes.

I kiss her soft forehead for the third time.

I leave the bedroom, closing the door, and I call Reid.

"Yeah, Leif?" he says breathlessly.

"Is Powers with you?"

"No, I assumed he was still with you. I've been trying like hell to get up to Brindley's apartment but the cops aren't letting me. They won't let anyone else go up until forensics gets here, and I'm about ready to roll some heads. I'm so fucking pissed, Leif. I hired the best people out there. Can you get back there?"

"I can't leave Kelly. I'll explain everything in the morning. In the meantime, Powers is probably still passed out in Brindley's apartment."

"He couldn't take it?"

"He's probably a rookie." I sigh. "I know you feel you have to, but if I were you, I wouldn't go up there. You don't want to see that sight."

"No, I don't. But I have to go up there. I have to know all

the results of my father's malice. Of his psychopathy. How else can I help these women?"

"Reid, you can help these women without seeing that. It's bad enough that you're probably going to have to see crime scene photos."

"Leif, I've made up my mind. This is my responsibility, and I have to take ownership. Besides, someone has to see to Officer Powers."

"Forensics will see to Powers. Take my advice. Don't go up there."

"I'm going."

I sigh. I can't talk him out of it. "Go at your own risk. Whoever was pounding on our door earlier is clearly the same person who did this to Brindley. He left a letter for Kelly. Her fingerprints will be on it because she opened it and read it. But I'd like to see if we can run other fingerprints on it."

"Absolutely. I'll send forensics to your place to pick it up."

"Are they here yet?"

"Not yet."

"All right. Doesn't matter anyway. No way am I getting any sleep tonight."

I check in on Kelly. Her eyes are closed. I don't know if she's asleep or not, but I don't want to disturb her, so I close the door quietly, sit down on the couch, and wait for forensics.

I JERK UPWARD at a knock on the door.

Damn. I must've fallen asleep. Unreal. Sometimes the body just gives out when the mind can't take it anymore.

I check my watch. Two a.m. It's probably forensics for the letter.

I go to the door, look out of the peephole. As I expected, it's Reid, a uniformed officer, and two others.

Reid looks about like I imagined he would after seeing the grisly sight of Brindley's murder—peaked and nauseated.

I open the door.

"Hey, Leif," Reid says. "This is Officer Gerard, who you met downstairs, and Officers Ford and Mylan from forensics."

I hold the door open for them. "Come in. The letter's on the table. The white envelope and the yellow legal piece of paper."

The two forensics officers—one male and one female—are already gloved. They take both the letter and the envelope and bag them, sealing them.

"How is Officer Powers?" I ask.

"He's fine," Gerard says. "Rookies are like that sometimes."

"I understand. That was not a pleasant sight."

"No, it wasn't," Officer Mylan, the female, says, her voice trembling slightly. "I've seen a lot in this job, and I'm pretty sure that was the worst."

Reid runs his fingers through his hair, shaking his head. "It was my job to protect these women."

"Man, don't put this on yourself." I grip his shoulder.

He moves away from me, breaking my grip. I get it. He doesn't want any kind of comfort. Neither do I.

"How can I not? I promised these women they would be safe here, in this apartment building."

"You put all possible precautions in place," I tell him. "This is not your fault, Reid."

"Of course it is. Someone got by security. Someone drugged the front officer, and we still haven't located the other two." Reid says nothing more, simply shakes his head and sighs.

"We're going to need to speak to Ms. Taylor in the morning," Officer Gerard says.

"Do you have to?" I ask. "She's been through so much. I think she's asleep now, but she's not going to be in any condition to talk to anyone in the morning."

"I'm sorry," Ford says, "but it must be done. She's going to be our major source of information in this case. We'll need to know who she thinks the perpetrator is. And why."

"No way. No. You will not make her relive those experiences on the island. I won't allow it."

I heard the ridiculousness of my words. Of course they must question Kelly. She's the only link to whoever did this.

"Leif..." From Reid, his face still stricken with regret and sadness.

"It won't happen, Reid. Kelly has been through way too much. The guilt she's feeling right now over Brindley... She asked me to lock her in a fucking closet, for God's sake. You understand what that means?"

"No," Reid says. "I don't."

"It means her mother used to do that to her. This poor woman has been abused her whole life, and I won't have her subjected to the torture of reliving it all."

"I'm afraid that's not your call," Gerard says.

"Kelly will want to help find this person," Reid says. "The

person who murdered Brindley, and who was threatening her. She wants to help the police."

"Yes, of course she will. But can it wait? She was so distraught after hearing about Brindley that she was bordering on delusional. She's a mess."

"Seems to me Mr. Wolfe here told me you were a SEAL," Gerard says.

"Yeah. So?"

"Then you know it has to be right away. This is murder, Mr. Ramsey, and Ms. Taylor is our only hope of finding this psychopath. We have to question her while everything's as fresh in her mind as possible."

He's right, of course. I'm being overprotective. Then again, isn't that what I'm paid for?

"She's going to need to be at the station tomorrow morning," Gerard says. "Ten a.m. sharp."

My body tenses, and I make two fists. I count to ten. All the fucking way to ten.

"Fine," I say through gritted teeth. "She will be there. And she will be with me."

"I'll arrange for counsel to go with you," Reid says.

"Why would we need counsel?"

"Trust me," Reid says. "I've found in these situations that it's always best to have counsel present."

"I'll make sure she's there. Now if you'll excuse me, it's close to three in the morning, and apparently I have an appointment tomorrow." I scoff. "Make that today."

They leave, and I lock the door. Time to check on Kelly.

11

KELLY

I'm no longer scared of the closet. I'm used to the loneliness and isolation. I hate my mother so much that now, to be in the closet, away from her, is a respite that I relish.

Sometimes I fall asleep, but more often than not I don't, because on the occasion I happen to be asleep when my mother finally opens the door, I'm punished further.

"You were sleeping." She kicks me in my shin. "You were supposed to be reflecting on your bad behavior. So you stay in there, and you reflect."

Reflect on what? Many times I'm not sure what I've done because she doesn't make it very clear. This time, though, she didn't like the dinner I made. It was spaghetti with a sauce made from tomatoes and cheese. Those were the only ingredients I could find in the house to make a meal from. I thought it was good. Maybe I was just hungry.

I didn't eat lunch at school today because there was nothing to make a sandwich with and I didn't have money to buy my lunch. It's not the first time. It happens a couple times a month. Sometimes my teacher notices and gives me something to eat, but then I *have to assure her that everything's fine at home and there's no reason to call my mother. I simply forgot my lunch.*

She didn't notice today, anyway.

Why should she? She has thirty students to take care of. Plus, she's not always in the cafeteria when we're eating.

But that's not reflecting, so I reflect. I'm a bad girl. Bad girls probably don't deserve to eat every day.

I sit here, alone in the closet, brushing my arms against the chill. It's wintertime, and though I'm wearing long sleeves, heat doesn't make it into the closet.

So I shiver, and I wait, and I try to do what my mother asks— reflect upon my bad behavior and learn something from it.

Each time, I do this.

And each time...nothing changes.

Because this is what bad girls deserve.

Sometimes I say it out loud.

Help myself believe it.

"This is what bad girls deserve."

One time I even yelled it.

"This is what bad girls deserve!"

SOMEONE IS SHAKING ME.

"Kelly! Kelly, wake up!"

My eyes pop open.

"This is what bad girls deserve!" I yell.

"Kelly, look at me." Strong hands cup my cheeks.

The lights are on in the bedroom, and the blue eyes... Those beautiful blue eyes are burning into mine.

Leif.

"This is what bad girls deserve," I say, softly this time.

"My sweet baby." He presses his lips to mine in a gentle kiss.

"This is what—"

He touches two fingers to my lips, quieting me. "I never want to hear you say that again."

I look around the bedroom—Leif's bedroom. That's right. Now I remember.

I'm here, and Brindley's dead, and The Dark One is coming after me.

Because this is what bad girls deserve.

"Don't ever say that again," Leif repeats.

"But—"

"I mean it, Kelly. None of this is your fault. None of it, do you hear me?"

I nod.

I nod to placate him.

I've heard this before. From Macy. From the therapists and counselors at the retreat center.

I was almost beginning to believe.

But now…

How can I ever believe it?

I drop my gaze from his, place my hands over his, and slide them from my cheeks.

"Kelly…"

"I won't say it."

"Good. Because it's not true. You're wonderful. And Kelly" —he tips my chin up until I meet his gaze once more—"I love you, baby."

I cock my head, squint a little.

And I remember…

Leif said those words before, when he put me to bed.

I look at him. At this beautiful man who just said words to me that I've never heard before. Are we together again? Didn't we end it?

"Why?" I ask.

He trails a finger over my upper lip and then my lower. "How can I not?"

"I can answer that easily." I grab a pillow and pull it onto my lap. "Because I don't deserve anything good in my life. Bad girls get what they deserve. They get locked in the closet. They get sent to islands where they're made to do horrible things. Then they wrongly accuse people of doing something awful, only to have that person die before they can tell her how sorry they are."

"Oh, baby, my poor baby..."

"Brindley..."

"Brindley knows how sorry you are, Kelly. Wherever she is now, she knows. I promise you."

"But —"

"Don't you dare tell me again that this is your fault. It's not."

"I want to believe that, Leif. I want to believe it so much."

"Then believe it. And believe that I love you, Kelly. And I swear to you, no one will harm you on my watch."

I fall against him then, and I let go.

All those tears that I've been holding back come in abundance, and I cry into Leif's shoulder. All the while he smooths my hair, soothes me, whispers to me how much he loves me.

And I cry...

I cry for the little girl in the closet who thought it was what she deserved.

I cry for the grown woman being held by Leif Ramsey who still thinks it's what she deserves.

I love you.

Leif said those words to me. Is saying those words to me.

And I want to say them back. I want to mean them. But I don't even know what love is. Is it the flutters in my tummy when I see Leif? Is it the jealousy I feel when I think of him with another woman? Is it the longing I feel when he's not with me? Is it the passion and desire I feel when we have sex? Or is it the pure comfort and nurturing I feel in his arms right now?

And it dawns on me, as if I've known it this whole time.

It's all those things.

Every single one and infinitely more.

It's...love.

I love this man. I love Leif Ramsey. I don't ever want to let him go.

12

LEIF

My God, I love this woman. I would gladly give my life for this woman. She's beautiful, intelligent, and so full of spirit. Yet she's insecure, still that scared little girl in many ways.

She's all that matters to me. I love her, and I'm never letting her go.

She cries into my shoulder, sometimes mumbling something unintelligible, but more often than not simply sobbing.

I will hold her for as long as it takes, I will protect her from anything that means her harm, and I will be at her side in the morning at her interview with the police.

I will protect her at all costs.

I hold her, caress her back, her arms, the top of her head.

For as long as she needs, I will hold her. Time passes—minutes, I don't know how many—until she finally pulls back a bit, her nose and eyes swollen and red, her cheeks stained from her tears.

"My baby..." I touch her cheek.

"Do you mean it, Leif? When you say you love me?"

"With all my heart."

"Are we together? Again? Were we ever?"

"If you want to be. If you don't want to be, that's okay too. I'll love you no matter what."

She bites her lip. "I want to say it back."

Emotion coils in my belly. I feel like a schoolboy again. But I remain calm. "You don't have to. Only if you feel it, Kelly. And if you don't, I'll survive."

"But I *do* feel it." She rubs her eyes. "At least, I think I do. I feel something I've never felt before, Leif. And it's… It's so many things. It's wonderful, yet it almost hurts. It's an ache. A yearning ache."

I smile. Because even though the events of tonight have been horrific, and I know we will be dealing with them for weeks to come, Kelly's description of what she feels for me touches my soul.

"That's love," I say.

"Are you sure?"

"I'm sure because it sounds an awful lot like what I feel for you, Kelly."

"Have you felt it before?"

"To a lesser degree, yes."

She tenses.

"Most people feel love for others before they find the one," I say.

"I haven't."

"I know you haven't, baby. I'm so sorry you didn't get that chance. But I love you, Kelly." I cup both her cheeks, almost gripping them, so that her lips smash together vertically. "I love you so much, and I don't care how long I have to wait for you to be ready to receive my love. I'll wait two years or twenty years, because I know in my heart that there is no one in the world for me except you."

A squeak comes from her throat.

"I mean it, baby. You're my forever."

"I love you," she says on a sigh. "If what I'm feeling is love, then I love you too, Leif."

My heart flies. Soars right out of my chest and into her, and I swear our two beating hearts become one.

I lower my mouth to hers, kiss her gently.

But gentle isn't what's on her mind. She parts her lips and probes into my mouth with her tongue.

I open for her, and this kiss...

To say it's one of passion would be an understatement. To say it's raw and primal isn't enough either.

It's...love. Pure and simple.

It's love in the form of a kiss.

After what she's been through, I don't want to ask her to make love, but that seems to be where she's heading.

Our lips are fused together, our tongues dueling, and she fingers the buttons of my shirt. She unbuttons me frantically and brushes the shirt from my shoulders.

Then her touch. Her hands are everywhere, caressing my shoulders, my neck, my pecs. Thumbing my nipples, sending a current of electricity through me.

But I need to be sure this is what she wants.

I break the kiss with a loud smack.

She wipes her lips with the back of her hand, raises her eyebrows at me.

"Kelly, it's the middle of the night. You need your sleep."

"I need you, Leif. I... I can hardly believe it. I can hardly believe that you love me."

I smile. "Believe it. I do."

She moves toward me but then pulls back and frowns. "I want to ask you how. Why? But you've already answered those questions. Macy always says I have to believe people at face value. It's so hard for me to do."

"Well, are you positive that you love me?"

"Yes. I am. If you say what I'm feeling is love—"

"No, Kelly. It's not what I say." I place my hand on her breast, right over her heart. "It's what you feel."

She smiles then, and even with her swollen nose and eyes and red tear-streaked cheeks, she's the most beautiful thing I've ever seen.

"It is what I feel. I've wondered if it was love. It's so wonderful that it threatens to squeeze my heart."

"Baby. As I told you, that sounds like love to me."

She cups my cheek, scrapes her fingers against my stubble. "Then I love you, Leif Ramsey. You are the first person in my life I've ever loved."

"I hope I'll be the last."

"You will be."

"I mean the last person in this way." I kiss her forehead. "You're allowed to love your friends. You're allowed to love the children we'll have."

Her eyes widen. "Children?"

My blood goes a little cold. "Yeah, probably too soon to bring that up."

"No. I mean... If you want children with me, that must mean..."

I know exactly what I mean, but I'm not sure she's ready to hear it. She needs to continue healing, and now with Brindley's murder, that path will be all the rockier. Then again? She needs to hear how much she means to me. To know that she's worthy of all the love I want to give her.

"It means I want to marry you, Kelly. I want to be your husband, and I want you to be my wife. That's all in the future, baby. You're not ready for any of that yet. We'll go as slow as you need to go. We have our whole lives together."

She drops her mouth open.

I tip her chin to bring her lips together. "What?"

"It's just... When you said *our whole life,* it made me feel... Even with every horrible thing that happened tonight... For the first time, Leif, I'm actually looking forward to my life."

My heart breaks a little.

This beautiful, vibrant woman doesn't know what love feels like, and now that she's embracing it, she's looking forward to life for the first time. How very wonderful...and how very sad.

"My God, baby..."

"Please don't take that the wrong way. I was never suicidal, Leif."

"Thank God."

"I just...existed. I existed in a state of resignation. I didn't fight for anything. Not even on the island. I was forced to run, to submit, to supposedly fight for my life, but I never thought my life would actually end."

"Right. Reid told me about that. The men weren't allowed to kill you."

"It wasn't even that, really. Every once in a while a woman would disappear with no explanation. We always assumed one of the guests had taken it too far. Even then, though, I didn't want my life to end, and I always fought hard when I had to. But I had accepted life as it was. I wasn't looking for anything more."

"God, Kelly. You're something."

"Because I don't want to die? I think that's pretty common."

He pulls me close. "That's not what I mean, although I'm glad you never felt you wanted to die. I mean that after everything you've been through, after living a life devoid of emotion, you're finally letting yourself feel. Some people go through their whole lives without ever allowing themselves to feel."

"I don't know if it's that I *did* let myself feel. I just didn't know. I didn't have any frame of reference for any of this."

"Now you do. Now you know what love is, Kelly Taylor, and I'm going to make sure you never forget."

13

KELLY

He kisses me.

It's a drugging kiss — a soul-crushing kiss. Both his hands are around my cheeks, and I feel his passion.

I feel his love.

He slides his hands over my hips and underneath my sweatshirt, and his touch sets me on fire.

He breaks the kiss long enough to pull the shirt over my head, and my breasts fall gently against my chest.

He lets out a groan, and then he slides his lips over my neck, my shoulder, across my chest, until he kisses a nipple. Just kisses it, and it makes me insane.

He's back to my mouth then, and the kiss is firm and open-mouthed and perfect in every way.

We kiss and we kiss and we kiss. I slide my hands over his warm neck and chest while he shoves my pants over my hips, brings them down, and then removes his jeans. We're naked on the bed. I'm lying on my back as he hovers over me, and I bring one leg up over his hips. He kisses my nipples, sucking one into his mouth, tugging on it, and then he lets it go with a soft pop as he glides his tongue between my breasts. He takes the other nipple between his lips while playing with the first one with his fingers.

I gasp. I moan. I cry out his name.

And I know... I know that he does this not just for his own pleasure but for mine as well.

A first for me. Knowing that the man touching my body isn't just doing it for himself.

I let out a whimper when he releases both my nipples, but then he pulls me up so that I'm sitting and he kisses me again. He kisses me with lots of tongue. Lots of lips. Lots of love and passion. Then he lets my lips go and I stare at him. Stare at his porcelain chest, his light-brown nipples, his perfect male beauty.

I lie back down, settle my head on the pillow, and slowly he spreads my legs.

My pussy is throbbing, waiting for his tongue, but instead he paints soft kisses all over my inner thighs, taking care to kiss each one of my scars.

They don't disgust him.

He spends a lot of time on them, as if he's healing them with his lips and his love.

But then...

Then he spreads my legs and slides his tongue over my pussy.

I gasp out in pleasure. "Oh, Leif!"

I close my eyes, undulate my hips, moving in tandem with his velvety tongue.

He eats me. He eats my pussy, and this body. This body is

mine. It never belonged to anyone else, no matter how many times it was violated. It's mine.

And I willingly give it to Leif.

His tongue... His tongue over my folds, over my clit, he moves it rapidly, driving me crazy, and I'm inching toward a climax...

He tugs on my clit, sucks on it, and my hands wander up my body, cupping my breasts, pinching my nipples.

Still he licks my pussy, concentrating on my clit. Until he moves forward, replacing his tongue with his fingers, and he kisses me. He kisses me deeply, and I taste my own juices on his lips and tongue.

I don't think he's ever tasted better when he kissed me.

It's the taste of life, of his tongue, of the inside of his mouth, which is always minty fresh. But it's also the taste of me, of the tang of my pussy.

And it's fucking glorious.

He breaks the kiss then, slides back to my body, giving each nipple a quick nip, and then kissing my belly, my abdomen, the top of my vulva, before he slides his tongue between my legs once more.

I'm on the brink of orgasm, just on the brink, but he's so good at sliding his tongue over me, bringing me almost to the precipice and then easing away. He's a tease, my Leif, but I'm enjoying every minute of it.

He licks my slit, and then he comes back to kiss me again. Another deep and full kiss, and he tastes even better this time. His fingers slide through my pussy folds, rub my clit. I'm so ready to come. So ready to come.

But then I look at him.

I look at him when he breaks the kiss, take in his beautiful Nordic features, his searing blue eyes, his light-blond hair. I find myself wanting to do something I've never wanted to do.

I want to touch him...down there.

I want to give him the pleasure that he's given me.

He moves us so we're side to side, and I melt against his chest, kiss his flat nipples, relishing the fact that they get hard for me as mine do for him. I rain kisses over his abs, tracing his sixpack with my tongue.

His skin is so warm, and I move back up to his mouth and kiss him. And then I touch him.

I wrap my hand around his hard cock.

God, it's hot. So hot, and now I know why I felt so cleansed the first time we fucked.

His cock is made of burning flames. And it's hard. So fucking hard.

I maneuver us so he's lying on the bed, and then I spread his legs and position myself between them.

He's huge. I'll never be able to take all of him, but I'll do my best. Because this is what I want. To please him. To please him the way he pleases me.

I slide my tongue over the head of his cock first, tasting the salty pre-come. I lick him all the way down to his balls. Back up and back down again.

Before I have a chance to take him into my mouth fully, he pulls me forward, kisses me passionately, and then pulls me into his arms, still not breaking the kiss.

He slides a finger into my pussy, and I nearly come right there.

Then he removes the finger and he's beside me. He nudges his cock at my entrance.

He kisses me, and then slides me onto my side so we're spooning, and he shifts his cock into me.

"Oh God..." I moan.

He pulls my face around to kiss me. Nibbles on my earlobe. I hold my thigh up so he can get a better angle and thrust more deeply.

The sensations...

As he burns through me, as he completes me...through my closed eyes I see the passion of our love.

I inhale the smell of our sex. Then I turn and look into his eyes. They're heavy-lidded, out of focus, as he continues to push into me.

God, his hands on my breasts, squeezing my nipples. And then his lips on my cheek, kissing me, tugging on my earlobe, all the while thrusting, thrusting, thrusting.

He pulls my face toward him again, kisses my lips, tangles his tongue with mine.

With my upper hand I reach behind me, touch his taut ass, push on it, hoping to get him farther and farther inside me.

I love you.

The words are in my head, surrounded by a lovely pink cloud.

I love you, I love you, I love you.

I'd say them except his tongue is in my mouth.

He pulls at me then, pulls us both over so that he's on his back and I'm on top of him. He positions me, pushes me down on his hard cock.

He doesn't even make me work, though I'd be glad to.

He holds my ass with his hands, holds me steady as he pumps into me, gyrating his hips.

So perfect.

We kiss for a while, and then he pinches my nipples.

I can't help myself. I have to move my hips, so I do. We thrust together in tandem, as our lips meet and are fused together.

All the times with Leif before, I enjoyed myself immensely.

But this? Now I know what making love truly is.

Now I know that it's not just a euphemism for fucking.

It's something truly distinct all on its own.

I pull myself upward, my hair in sweaty strands around my cheeks and shoulders. Leif pushes it back, cupping my cheeks.

"Look at me, my beautiful Kelly."

I meet his gaze as I suck the thumb of one of his hands into my mouth.

His eyes are searing blue, and they're not just gazing into mine, they've become magnetically pulled to mine.

"Yes, Kelly, baby. Look at me. Watch my eyes, watch my lips, listen to these words as I say them to you." He thrusts again, gritting his teeth. "I love you, baby. I love you, Kelly Taylor. Always."

I sigh, never letting my gaze fall from his. He's still thrusting into me, and I grip his shoulders for support. "I love you too, Leif. I love you so much."

Then I fall forward and lock lips with his.

We're still fucking.

No, not fucking. Making love, and—

Leif breaks the kiss. "Touch yourself, Kelly," he says. "Touch yourself and make yourself come. For me."

Touch myself?

I've tried it before. It doesn't work.

But it will tonight. It will work while Leif is embedded in my body.

Our gazes never wavering, I bring myself forward until I'm perpendicular to him, his cock deep inside me.

He cups my breast, twists my nipples, and I gasp, electricity flowing through me.

I slide my hand down my abdomen to touch my clit, and

—

"God, yes!"

The orgasm rips through me, unlike anything I've ever experienced before.

It's intense, it's raw, animalistic, yet it's passionate and filled with promise.

Filled with love.

"That's it, Kelly. God, you're beautiful when you come. Keep going, baby, keep going. I want you to come long and hard for me."

"Yes," I breathe out. "God, yes." The climax subsides and then begins again.

I sigh, deep in the nirvana of orgasm, as Leif continues thrusting, thrusting, thrusting...

"Keep coming, Kelly," he says through clenched teeth. "Keep coming because I'm— Oh!" he grunts out.

He pushes up into me, filling me so completely, and as my orgasm slides downward, I feel it. I feel his release. Every pulse of it.

I don't move.

I can't move.

I want to sit here forever, right on top of Leif's cock,

because this feeling of completion... It will fade as soon as he moves out of me.

When his pulses finally subside, he tugs on my hands, pulling me down. "Come here, baby. Come. Kiss me, my love."

Our lips meet, our bodies still joined, and love... Love flows around us.

And I know that it's love. I know it in my heart and my soul.

14

LEIF

K issing Kelly...
Making love with Kelly...
Words flow through my head, trying to describe something that's indescribable...

Passionate, fulfilling, perfect in every way. Beautiful, like a sunrise, like the beginning of a new day where everything goes smoothly.

Pure perfection.

Nirvana.

Heaven.

Paradise.

All good words, but none of them quite accurate.

There's not a word that exists to describe the pure happiness I'm feeling at this moment.

My dick stays hard, embedded inside her, as we continue kissing.

Normally it would be going down by now, but it shows no signs of that.

I gently maneuver us so that we're both lying on our sides, facing each other as we continue the kiss.

It's a gentle kiss now, a kiss of completion, a kiss of love, a kiss of the future.

For this woman is my future. I won't pressure her. She still needs more healing, and I understand and respect that.

So we continue to kiss, and kiss, and kiss...

Until we both fall off into gentle slumber.

I'M jolted awake by my phone alarm at eight in the morning.

Shit.

Kelly's appointment at the police station. Ten a.m. sharp.

And I forgot to tell her about it.

I know what to expect. She will revert to old Kelly, tell me where to get off—and in this case she has a good argument. I should have remembered to tell her.

I rise, the sun streaming through the slatted blinds. Then I turn and look at the beautiful woman still lying in my bed.

She's naked, the sheet between her legs.

Her lips are still red and swollen from all our kissing, and the smell of sex as I inhale is still thick in the room.

God, I hate to wake her.

She hardly got any sleep last night, and I know she has to work tonight.

But after what happened with Brindley, and now with the questioning she's going to endure and the horrific message she received...

Surely her new boss will be understanding...

I don't know.

But if she's not? I don't give a shit. Kelly will get another job. A better job.

I head to the bathroom, take care of business, slide on my jeans, and go to the kitchen to start some coffee. First, I'll make Kelly a nice breakfast. Bacon, eggs, toast, and pancakes.

Does she like those things?

Damn. I'm in love with this woman, but I don't even know what she likes to eat. I know she likes pizza, and she likes a turkey and avocado sandwich.

Pancakes seem like the safest choice. I grab some pancake mix and milk and get started.

A few moments later, just as the coffee is done brewing, I have a stack of six pancakes. I grab the bottle of maple syrup, a stick of butter, and put everything out on the table.

Then I go to wake up Kelly.

She's moved a little. She's now on her side, tangled up in the gray sheet.

She looks like an angel. An auburn angel, with her hair splayed out on the pillow.

I touch her shoulder gently. "Kelly."

She doesn't respond at first, so I nudge a bit harder.

"Kelly."

Her eyes open sleepily. "Hey."

"I made breakfast. You like pancakes?"

"With raspberry syrup?" she asks.

"Maple syrup."

"That's a decent second." She sits up in bed, stretching her arms over her head with a yawn.

"Everything's on the table. All I need is you."

"Okay. Give me a minute." She rises and goes into the bathroom while I head back out to the kitchen.

A few minutes later, she's back in her sweatpants and sweatshirt, and she sits down at the table, inhaling. "Smells great. Buttery."

I smile. "That would be the butter. How do you take your coffee?"

"Just black."

"Good. Me too." I fill both of our cups from the coffeepot that I placed on the table.

I wait until she's eaten a good portion of her breakfast before I bring up the inevitable.

"Kelly..."

"Yeah?"

"I love you."

She smiles shyly. "I love you, too."

I clear my throat. "There's something I should've mentioned last night."

Her eyes widen. "Oh my God. You forget to use a condom or something?" She wrinkles her forehead. "I suppose it doesn't matter. I've got one of those implants. They made us have them on the island, and I decided to keep mine until... Well, you know. I'm not ready for anything like that."

I reach across the table and squeeze her hand. "No, I didn't forget to use a condom. But it's nice to know we don't need one from now on."

"You're clean?"

"Yep. Besides, believe it or not, I haven't had sex with anyone else in six months."

"Good."

"I figured you'd like that. But I do have to tell you something."

"What is it?"

"I have to take you to the police station this morning at ten. They want to question you."

This time her jaw drops, and her fork clatters to the floor.

"I meant to tell you last night, baby. You were so distraught, and then... Well, you know what happened."

"Why?"

"Because of the message. The letter. And...Brindley."

"But I didn't have anything to do with any of that."

"I know. The cops just need to get every bit of information that they can. I can go with you. And Reid said he'd have an attorney—"

"An attorney?" she gasps.

"Calm down, baby. It's just a formality. Reid wants to make sure you're protected. This is just questioning."

"What if they arrest me?"

"For what, Kelly? You haven't done anything wrong."

She closes her mouth then, inhales deeply.

Then she closes her eyes, inhales through her nose and out through her mouth three times.

When she opens her eyes, she meets my gaze. "I'm tired, Leif. I have to work tonight."

"I know, baby. I tried telling the cops all that last night, but they want to get a jump on things, and I can't blame them. Once we find out who's behind this, you won't have to worry anymore."

"You said you'd protect me."

"I did say that, and I will, but the best protection is for whoever's threatening you to be safely locked behind bars... or six feet under."

∾

KELLY and I are both dressed up for the questioning. She wears her work attire of black pants and white blouse, and I look pretty much the same, black dress pants, white button-down, and this time I added a navy-blue tie.

Her hair is pulled back in a classy French braid, while mine is a mess like it always is, but my clothes are neatly pressed, and I think I look okay.

The attorney Reid sent is none other than Lacey Ward Wolfe herself, Rock's wife. She looks wonderful, of course, also very professional with her blond hair pulled back into a tight bun, and a navy-blue suit that shows her burgeoning baby bump.

"I can't believe Reid sent you," I say.

"Rock and Reid want the best for all of their father's victims"—her cheeks flush—"and I guess they think I'm the best."

"Do you have any criminal law experience?" Kelly asks.

"Only a little," Lacey says, "but I'm well versed in dealing with routine police questioning. Besides, there's no reason to believe that any criminal proceedings will come out of this, Kelly. You haven't done anything wrong. This is just routine questioning, and trust me, I won't let it get out of hand."

Kelly simply nods, her hands clasped in her lap and her knuckles white. Her usual stance when she's tense.

I want to grab her hand, offer her comfort, but I don't know if she's comfortable with us going public with our relationship, so I keep my hands to myself.

Before long, we're led back to one of the interrogation rooms.

I've been in these rooms many times before, mostly for things pertaining to the Wolfe family.

They're bare and sterile, with an oblong table, where the officer sits on one side, and the person being questioned, along with any others, sits on the other side.

The uniformed officer opens the door, and a young woman with blond hair and brown eyes rises and walks over to us. "I'm Detective Castella," she says, holding out her hand. "You must be Ms. Taylor."

Kelly's hands remain at her side. "Yes."

Shake her hand. I try to reach her telepathically. I know she didn't hear my thought, but she does finally hold out her hand and places it in Detective Castella's.

Lacey sticks her hand out next. "I'm Lacey Wolfe, attorney for Ms. Taylor, and this is Leif Ramsey, a contractor with Wolfe Enterprises."

"Nice to meet all of you." Detective Castella shakes Lacey's hand and then mine. She gestures to the table. "Please, have a seat."

I help by pulling out the middle chair for Kelly, and then Lacey and I each sit beside her, flanking her with our protection.

"All right, let's get down to business." Detective Castella taps on her laptop, and then opens the manila folder sitting on the table. "Ms. Taylor, what can you tell me about Brindley McGregor?"

Kelly clears her throat. "Not much, I'm afraid."

"I apologize for bringing up this terrible part of your past, but you knew her on Derek Wolfe's island?"

"I knew who she was, yes. But none of us really knew each other on that island."

"Detective," Lacey interjects, "if you want information about the women on the island, I can refer you to Macy

Banks, the therapist for the women. She will back up what Kelly says. The women did not interact with each other much on the island."

"Yet I understand that you thought Ms. McGregor was sending you threatening texts," Castella says.

"I was mistaken." Kelly drops her gaze to the tabletop.

Damn, Kelly. Look the woman in the eye.

She still looks at the table, though.

Kelly doesn't know about body language, but I do. We were well trained in it in the Navy. How to read someone. And when you don't look an interrogator in the eye? They think you're lying.

Kelly's not lying, but her body language says that she is.

"And how did you find out that you were mistaken?"

"Brindley denied it, although I didn't believe her at first. But I finally believed her."

"What made you believe her?"

"The last text I got. It came while I was in her presence, and it contained some of the same language in the letter that Leif said he gave you. I believe the texts are coming from a man from the island."

"I see. Which man?"

"I don't know his name." Kelly lets out a scoff.

Easy, Kelly.

"What did he call himself?"

"Mr. Smith."

Castella rolls her eyes.

"I'm not lying to you. He called himself Mr. Smith."

Oh God...

"I didn't accuse you of lying, Ms. Taylor."

"You rolled your eyes."

"Yes. I rolled my eyes because Mr. Smith as an alias is a little on the nose, don't you think?"

Kelly opens her mouth but no words come out.

"Let's continue," Lacey says. "Ms. Taylor had a rough night last night and we should get this over with as soon as possible."

Lacey's voice is calm and direct. I get the feeling she's trying to send Kelly a subliminal message as well.

Whether she picks up on any of it... I inhale.

"Yes, of course." Detective Castella taps on her computer. "The preliminary report from forensics shows only one set of fingerprints on the letter in question."

"I'm afraid those will be mine," Kelly says. "I opened the letter and touched it."

"And a spot of blood," Castella says.

Kelly holds out her left hand, showing the paper cut on her thumb. "I cut myself on the flap of the envelope as I was opening it."

"So what you're saying is that those fingerprints are yours, and if we analyze the blood, it will show that it is yours as well."

"Yes. I am the one who opened the letter. And I did bleed on it."

I grow tense.

I don't like this line of questioning from Detective Castella. Surely she can't think...

"Mrs. Wolfe," she says to Lacey, "it's my understanding that your husband and your brother-in-law have traced all of the text messages that have come to Ms. Taylor, correct?"

"That's correct," Lacey affirms.

"And they were all untraceable?"

"Also correct."

"Ms. Taylor, have you ever purchased a burner phone?"

Kelly's eyes go wide.

"You don't have to answer that, Kelly," Lacey says. "Detective Castella, that question is irrelevant."

"I find it very relevant."

"The answer won't lead to anything productive. At best it would be circumstantial. People buy burner phones all the time for hundreds of reasons."

"I would like for Ms. Taylor to answer the question."

"Kelly—"

"No," Kelly interrupts Lacey. "I've never purchased a burner phone. I don't even know where I would find a burner phone."

Tension threads through the room, so thick that I can feel it.

Lacey is now as tense as I am.

We both know exactly why Detective Castella asked the question, and we're not happy about it.

"You can easily find places to purchase a burner phone online," Castella says.

"Why would I do that when I've had no reason to purchase one?" Kelly asks.

Castella taps on her computer again. "I can never know exactly what you and your friends went through on that island."

"They're not my friends," Kelly says.

"They're not?"

"I just told you. We didn't really interact with each other on the island."

"What about at the retreat center, after you were rescued?"

"Do you really think any of us were in any condition to forge friendships?" Kelly's tone is harsh. "We had just been rescued from human slavery, Detective."

Oh, Kelly...

I understand where she's coming from, but she needs to be more cooperative. Again, I try to reach her subliminally, and again, I know it's an exercise in futility.

"All right." Castella clears her throat. "What I was trying to say is that I'll never understand what you went through on the island."

"No, you won't."

Another throat clear from Castella. She's trying to be patient, but I know from experience that Kelly can try anyone's patience. Even a saint's. And Detective Castella is no saint. She's going after Kelly, and she's wrong. All I can do is be here with Kelly for support.

"That being said," the detective continues, "there are some people who might believe you wrote this text yourself, Ms. Taylor."

Kelly stands then and pounds her fist on the table. "I did not! Install a fucking camera in my apartment if you want to. Watch me every minute of every fucking day. I've never bought a burner phone, and I've never sent a text to myself. Go ahead. Install a fucking camera. Why should I care? I've already got round-the-clock security, someone watching me every minute. Do you even know what that feels like? I may as well be a rat in a cage."

"Kelly..." I touch her forearm lightly.

"No, Leif. Can you believe this?"

"I don't believe it," Lacey says, also rising. "Detective, you are way out of line. To even suggest such a thing is reprehensible."

"Mrs. Wolfe, she just admitted that hers are the only fingerprints on that piece of paper."

"Yes, and she also just admitted that she opened it and read it. Even cut her finger on it. Did you have any reason to think you should put on rubber gloves before opening that letter, Kelly?"

"No, of course not," Kelly says through clenched teeth. "It was on Leif's table—"

"It wasn't in your own apartment?" Detective Castella interrupts.

"No. I was at Leif's apartment. He told me to stay there to stay safe."

"So you opened an envelope that clearly didn't belong to you."

Kelly gulps then.

"Actually, the envelope *did* belong to her," I interject. "You've read it yourself. It's a note to her. I'm sure you know the whole story of the pounding on Ms. Taylor's door last night. That envelope was dropped outside her door when I went out to try to see what it was. I stuffed it in my pocket, and when I left Ms. Taylor locked in my apartment, I put the envelope on the table."

"Still, Ms. Taylor, you had no way of knowing—"

"This is all completely irrelevant, Detective." Lacey raises her voice. "I believe we're done here."

"Very well." Detective Castella closes her laptop and then presses a button.

The officer opens the door. "Detective?"

"Please show Ms. Taylor and her companions out." Then she looks at Kelly. "And Ms. Taylor? Don't go anywhere. We're going to have more questions."

Once we're outside, out of earshot from anyone at the station, Lacey turns to Kelly.

"Kelly, you cannot go off like that during police questioning."

"Aren't you supposed to be my lawyer?"

"Yes, but you didn't let me get a word in edgewise. If you had, you would've known not to answer those questions."

"Not answering makes me look guilty."

"No, it doesn't. And your guilt is irrelevant at this point. You're not accused of anything."

I can't help interjecting then. "I'm sorry, Lacey, but it sure did sound like that woman was accusing Kelly of sending those texts herself."

"She was using classic questioning tactics," Lacey says. "Kelly, if you had listened to me in the first place, she wouldn't have even gotten to ask questions."

Kelly opens her mouth and already I can hear something caustic coming out of it. I wince, waiting for her fiery words.

They don't come. She closes her mouth.

Thank God.

"Let's get you back to the apartment," I say. "You need some rest."

And for once...she doesn't fight me.

15

KELLY

"You sure you don't want to call in to work?" Leif asks me once we're back at my apartment.

"No." I shake my head. "How would that look? It's only my second day."

"I know, but the manager already made it clear that she's sympathetic to your situation."

"I don't want anyone's sympathy, Leif. I just want..." I bite down on my lip to keep from crying.

"I know." He kisses my cheek. "I love you."

The words warm me. That feeling of rainbows and sunshine that I've never felt before infuses me with strength.

"I love you too." I meet his gaze and then look away. "Part of me still can't believe that you love me."

"Honestly? Part of me still can't believe it either."

I scoff. "And what the hell is that supposed to mean?"

He pushes a strand of hair behind my ear. "Not what you think it means. It means I never expected to fall in love so quickly. Not with you, not with anyone."

"Have you ever been in love before, Leif?"

"Just once."

I cross my arms. "I haven't."

"I know. I'm so sorry about that. I'm so sorry you've lived your life without love."

"Who was she?"

"The younger sister of my best friend during childhood. We were in high school, and she was two years younger."

"Did you..."

"Yeah." He laughs. "Let me tell you, it wasn't pretty."

"I see." I look down.

He takes my chin up. "Kelly, I'm over thirty years old. You didn't truly think I'd never had sex before you, did you?"

"As good as you are at it? No. But I'd like to pretend that it was only me."

"Hey, you asked the question."

"Yeah, but after I asked I realized I didn't really want to know the answer."

"Would you rather I lied to you?"

This time I get angry. "No. Absolutely not. I don't ever want you to lie to me, Leif. I'm so tired of lies and deception."

He cocks his head, trails a finger down my cheek. "Have others lied to you in the past?"

"Yes."

"Your mother?"

"Yeah. I mean, sometimes she said she loved me, but that was a big old lie because of the way she treated me. Actions speak louder than words." She pauses, twists her lips. "Though in her own head, I don't think she was lying. Like, for example, when she gave me a horrible present for my birthday, I think she really felt it was a good idea. In her own warped head."

"Oh God. What happened?"

In monotone, I relay the story. "I used to love to play volleyball. You've seen my tattoo."

"Yeah."

"It was my tenth birthday, and of course she had shoved me in the closet—"

"Wait. On your birthday?"

"It's a long story. I should've left that part out."

"I knew you had it bad, but— I guess if she's the kind of parent who shoves a kid in the closet, why would she make an exception on a birthday?"

"Just let me finish the story. Maybe one day I'll tell you everything."

He nods, playing with strands of my hair that have come loose from my French braid.

"Anyway, when she finally let me out of the closet, there was a present sitting at my place at the table. It was wrapped in plain red wrapping paper, but when I looked closer, it actually had a snowflake pattern in darker red on it. So she couldn't even buy birthday wrapping paper—"

He opens his mouth but I gesture him to stay quiet.

"That's not really important. Just something I remember."

"If you remember it, then it *is* important. Something that stayed with you. But anyway, go ahead."

I draw a breath. "So I open the present, and inside was"— I swallow against the lump in my throat—"my volleyball."

"A volleyball?"

"No. *My* volleyball, Leif. The volleyball I had scraped and saved for with my own money. So that I could have my own volleyball when I played with the other girls after school. It was deflated in a shoebox."

"She deflated your volleyball?"

"Not only that, she punctured it in several places so I couldn't reinflate it." My lips tremble. "It was ruined. She said I was spending too much time playing volleyball, and that she needed me here at home. And then she made me—" I swallow again. "She made me thank her, Leif. She made me thank her for such a thoughtful gift."

He pulls me to him. "Kelly," he says against my hair.

"So now you understand my tattoo. Volleyball made me happy. What I thought of as happy at that point. It gave me a break from my unsatisfying home life. And I was good at it. I mean, I probably never would've been as good as Aspen. But I liked it and I was good at it and I wanted to have my own volleyball. So I scrimped and saved and bought it, and she took it from me."

"Your tattoo..."

I nod against him.

My tattoo. The volleyball surrounded by wilted black roses.

"To remind me. To remind me that anything good that comes into my life is just going to be taken away. As if I needed reminding."

"My poor baby. After all you've been through, and then—the island."

I nod.

In a flash, a memory and image come into my mind. I've talked to Macy about that day, but I don't think about it a lot. I haven't healed from it.

But now...with Leif's love, I believe I have the strength to deal with it.

THE DAYS at the diner were always the same. My shift was breakfast and lunch. Six a.m. to two p.m., six days a week. Tuesdays were my days off.

Today, one of the servers, Catania, called in sick, and I was pulling double duty.

I didn't mind, though. Keeping busy kept my mind occupied, and I got double the tips. A win-win situation.

On top of that, the other server on duty—usually there were three of us at breakfast—Georgianna, got a phone call and asked me to cover her tables for a moment.

A nondescript man sat alone in one of Georgianna's booths. He was nearly finished with his meal.

"Good morning," I say to him. "Your server got a phone call, and she asked me to take care of you. Can I get you anything else, sir?"

He wipes his lips on his napkin and then sets it across his plate. "No, I think I'm good." He pulls out his wallet and sets several bills on the table. "Just my check, please."

"Right away, sir."

I head to the kitchen, grab the order for his table number, and then return to the cash register where I total his order and print out his check. I hurry back to the table—

But he's gone.

He left several bills on the table, enough to cover the check and leave Georgianna a hefty tip.

On top of the bills sits a piece of candy wrapped in foil.

All I did was bring his check, so I leave the entirety of the tip for Georgianna.

But I take the chocolate.

I unwrap it and pop it into my mouth.

Ah, the creaminess. It's a milk chocolate unlike anything I've ever tasted. Belgian chocolate, according to what is printed on the silver wrapper. I've never had anything so good in my mouth.

I do a quick check of the rest of my tables, and then take the order of some new customers seated in my area. As I'm turning the order in to the kitchen, my stomach churns.

I swallow.

All I had for breakfast was a piece of dry toast. Maybe I need to eat something. But I can't take a break with Georgianna's and my tables to deal with. I work through it. I work through the stomach pain and the nausea that comes as well, until—

I'm heading to a new table to take an order when I have to make a trip to the bathroom.

I make it into a stall and empty the dry toast and mostly stomach acid into the toilet.

God.

I must have caught whatever kept Catania from coming into work today.

I sit on the floor of the stall and wipe my mouth with toilet paper. I have to go back to work. Catania's out, Georgianna is still on a phone call. I'm all there is.

I have to go back to work.

I heave again into the toilet, and this time it's painful. I've already emptied my stomach, so it's nothing but dry heaves. When it finally subsides, sweat is trickling down my forehead.

I grip the edges of the toilet seat and attempt to stand, and then—

I wake up.

I wake up, naked, in a strange concrete room.

16

LEIF

This strong woman. Sometimes I can't believe I've knocked down part of her wall.

But there's so much more to go.

"I don't eat chocolate," she says into my shoulder.

"I know. You told me."

"I never talk about why I don't eat chocolate," she says. "But I think…"

I pull away from her a bit, meet her gaze. "What?"

"I can't be sure, but I think I was poisoned by chocolate. Chocolate that a customer at the diner left along with his payment for his check. The weird thing is, it wasn't even my table."

"What?"

"Yeah. I never really knew who was responsible for sending me to that island."

"I thought it might've been your mother."

"Yeah, the thought has crossed my mind. Did she really hate me that much?"

"I don't know. Only she can answer that question."

She sighs. "Yes. She did hate me that much, but how would she even know about the island?"

I place my arm around her shoulder. "Kelly, let's sit down. I need to tell you a little bit about your mother." I lead her to the couch, take her hand in mine. "I told you I met with her."

She pushes away from me. "Don't remind me."

"You know, she *does* want to see you."

"Yeah, I know. It's all an act. I will *not* see her."

"I know. I told her that."

"What the hell did she try to tell you? That I had some kind of idyllic childhood?"

"She alluded to that, yeah. I didn't believe her, of course. But that's not the main thing I need to tell you."

"What is it then?"

"Your mother came into some money about six months after you were taken. Before your aunt died."

Her eyes pop into circles. "You don't think..."

"No, I don't. I don't think she was the one who sold you out to the island. First of all, the money she came into was a huge amount. More than anyone else got for selling out their friends or family to that island."

"What did she get?"

"Two million dollars, paid over the course of a year."

"My mom is fucking rich?"

"Yeah. She got into some hot stocks at the time, and then, as you know, she had a rich aunt who died with no offspring, leaving your mother the entire estate."

"So what's she worth now?"

"Around thirty million or so."

Kelly's jaw drops. "I agree that she wasn't behind my

abduction. I can't believe anyone would pay two million just for me."

"I agree with you. I don't think that's where the money came from. The Wolfes are looking into it, but so far they haven't been able to track it."

"It was five years ago, and whoever did it wouldn't have left tracks," she says.

"Probably not, but they will uncover it, Kelly. I promise."

She sighs.

"Did your mother ever mention who your father was?"

"She said he was a one-nighter. She didn't even know his name. Then she told me he was dead. I don't know."

"We know one thing about him, probably," I say.

"What's that?"

"Clearly, your mother likes red hair. She colors her hair red, and your hair is red. So it's not outside the realm of possibility that your father had red hair."

"Great. So we're looking for a dead redhead."

"He may not be dead, Kelly. Is your mother known for telling the truth?"

"I don't know, Leif. I don't know the woman. I don't want to know the woman." She buries her head in her hands.

"I understand. But do you want to find out who sold you out?"

"I don't know. I never really thought about it before. My life has always been such crap, I just figured it was no worse than usual."

My heart hurts. As if a giant fist is squeezing it, trying to juice it.

This beautiful woman—with so much intelligence and cunning and love inside her—never thought she deserved anything better than to be held captive on an island and used and abused in the worst way.

"It might give you some closure if we found out," I say.

"Closure?"

"Yeah. Surely you've talked to Macy about closure."

"She's used that word before, but I've never really understood it. Closure from what? Closure from every bad experience of my life? Then I have nothing."

I tip her chin. "Please tell me that's not true."

She gives a small smile. "You're right. My time with you, Leif, but that's such a small fraction of the years I've lived."

"I promise you, baby, that our years together are going to eclipse all the horror in your life."

"If only..."

"Hey, love is a pretty powerful thing. It can help you heal. It can help you live."

"I've already been living. Except... That's not really true, is it? I've simply been existing."

"Exactly. Kelly, if you don't want to know who is responsible for your abduction, we can let it lie. I have a feeling... I have a feeling that once we find out who's been sending you these messages, things will begin to fall into place."

"I told you. I'm sure it's that man from the island. Mr. Smith."

"And it may well be. The Wolfes have the best people on it, and I will not stop until we've eliminated every threat to you. I promise you that."

A grin splits her pretty face.

"Let's get you to bed."

"Leif?"

"Yeah?"

"I... I don't want to stay here. In this place. He knows where I am."

She raises a good point. "You want to stay in my apartment?"

"Well...yes." She smiles shyly. "But no. It's right next door. It's not a big leap for him to find me there."

"You're right, but Reid has quadrupled the security here. He won't get in again."

"This all just happened last night. He can't have quadrupled security by now."

I pause a moment, stroke my jaw. "All the Wolfes have to do is throw around cash and they get things done. But I understand your reluctance. I could book us into a hotel, but hotels have almost no security. I'm not sure what to do."

"What about a different..." She shakes her head. "I don't know either."

"I'll tell you what. For now, let's get you settled at my place. I won't leave your side."

"Okay." She nods. "That's at least better than staying here."

"I should hope so." I kiss her forehead.

"Being with you will be wonderful, Leif. But you know what I meant."

"Yeah, I know. Sure I can't talk you out of skipping work tonight?"

"I can't believe you're even asking me to." She rakes her gaze over my body. "You're a military man. A man of honor, who always keeps his commitments."

"I absolutely do, and I respect the fact that you want to keep yours. But you haven't had any sleep, Kelly. Your safety is at issue here."

"Who's going to take me out of a busy restaurant?" She stops quickly as her eyes widen and the rosy color drains from her cheeks. "I was at the restaurant. Getting sick from the chocolate I ate. I tried to stand after throwing up, and then... A minute later I woke up naked in a concrete room."

"Oh, baby... So you see what I mean then."

"I do. But Leif, for the first time, I have a job that I'm good at and that's paying me something other than crap wages and shitty tips. I don't want to give it up."

"All right. But I'm going to be at the restaurant during your entire shift."

17

KELLY

True to his word, Leif has sat at a central table at The Glass House during my entire shift. When he arrived with me at work, he took Lois aside, and after that, he had a small central table to himself all night. He was in another server's section, which was just as well. I wouldn't have been able to concentrate if I had to serve him all night. I don't know what he offered to pay for use of the table for the entire shift, but with the Wolfes' money, I'm sure it was a nice sum.

He spent most of his time reading on his iPad. Or perhaps he was working. I don't know.

I didn't ask.

But I was happy that he was here.

The shift is finally over, and I'm dead on my feet.

Leif is still sitting at his table, his eyes on his iPad. He must be exhausted as well. He didn't get any more sleep than I did.

Most of the cleanup is done by the bussers, but I'm

expected to at least brush all the crumbs off my tables so they won't clog the washer when they're laundered.

I head to the break room and from there to the employees' restroom.

One look at the mirror tells the tale.

My eyes are heavy-lidded and bloodshot.

I fear I won't be able to get any more sleep tonight, because I'll be worrying constantly that The Dark One will appear.

I head into a stall, take a quick piss, and emerge and wash my hands. I grip the edge of the sink for a moment, closing my eyes.

Exhaustion weighs on me, and I'm bone tired. So bone tired.

But I can't fall asleep in the employee bathroom.

I have to at least wait until I get back to Leif's apartment, where I can fall asleep in his arms.

I open my eyes—

And I gasp, my heart jumping.

Behind me stands a man.

A man with dark hair and dark eyes...and a white mask covering most of his face.

I don't turn. Because I'm frozen. Frozen in time, my gaze locked on the mirror.

"Hello, Kelly." His voice is the same. Not deep so much as dark. "Did you think I wouldn't come for you?"

"How did you get in here?" My knuckles are white as I clutch the edge of the sink, not daring to turn around from my reflection. He's only in the mirror. An image in the mirror. Not real. A mirage.

Except it's not a mirage. Not a—

"I can get anywhere I need to be."

"Please," I rasp out. "Please go. Please just let me have my life."

"You don't understand, Kelly." He steps closer to my reflection. "I *want* you to have a life. A life with me."

"You..." My voice cracks. "You killed Brindley."

"I only do what I must," he says.

"She was no threat to you. She was so young."

"But you didn't like her, Kelly. You thought she was sending you the texts."

"I was mistaken."

"Were you?"

"I think that's clear, don't you?"

Then I shudder. I spoke harshly to him. He may not like that.

"There's the fiery Kelly I remember." His dark eyes burn into me through the silver glass of the mirror. "I never knew why they called you Opal. Opal is a gentle stone. That's not you."

"What do you want?"

"*You*, Kelly." He takes another step. "You were always mine."

"Then why did you choose others?" I can't help asking.

"Because of the way it affected you. I wanted to see your jealousy." He groans. "I liked it."

My God, this man is sick. He's sick and twisted, just like my mother.

"What is your name?" I ask.

He grins, his teeth light yellow against the stark white of his mask. "You know my name. I'm Mr. Smith."

"No." I will my voice to steady. "I want your real name."

"It's a little too soon for that."

"How can you say that? You say you want me, but you won't let me know who you are. How am I supposed to want you?"

"You already do. You proved that on the island."

I gulp. "Why aren't you in prison?"

"Because I'm smarter than the cops. Smarter than the Feds. And I have a lot of money."

"How much?"

"Enough. Enough that you'll never want for anything."

"Please. Just let me go."

He glances toward the door of the bathroom. "The time isn't right, but when I have things ready, I will come back for you. And remember..." He pulls a knife from his waistband and then gestures to the bulge in his pants. "One will go inside you. It's up to you which one. Goodbye."

He whisks out the doorway.

He has to go somewhere. He had to come from somewhere. Surely Leif will see him.

But my hands are glued to the edge of the sink, my knuckles tense, my heart trying to jump out of my chest.

I can't move. In fact, my breath... Can't get my breath...

Until I remember...and I inhale sharply.

I swallow against the nausea, but my stomach cramps up, and I throw up in the sink. The filet of sole that I had during my dinner break and all the coffee I drank to stay awake tonight.

I turn on the water, trying to force the chunks of fish down the drain, but to no avail. The sink is clogged.

I lose my footing, and I'm on the floor.

And that is when the tears come.

More tears.

Because now? Now I have something to lose.

18

LEIF

"Do you need anything else before I shut down the kitchen for good?" Lois, the manager, asks me.

"No, thank you. I'm just waiting for Kelly." I let out a giant yawn. "We've both been through some stuff and we haven't had a lot of sleep in the last twenty-four hours."

She clasps a hand to her mouth. "Goodness, why didn't you just call me? We would've gotten someone to fill in for Kelly tonight."

"I tried to get her to call in, but she wouldn't have any of it. She wants to do a good job for you. Since it's only her second night, she didn't feel comfortable asking for time off."

"She needn't feel that way," Lois says. "We all know what those women have been through. And the Wolfes are such good customers here."

"I know that, but she doesn't want any special treatment, and I respect her for that."

"Certainly, I do too. But I'll tell you what. Let me take a look at the schedule." She pulls her phone out of her pocket and opens her calendar app. "Yes, Kelly is supposed to work tomorrow, but I'm going to switch her to Sunday. I actually have another server who requested Sunday off, but I wasn't able to accommodate him. Now I can."

"That's so kind of you, but you should probably check with Kelly first."

"Really?"

"You know what? She won't like it, but I'll make an executive decision. Yes, please do change the schedule. Kelly needs some time to recuperate."

"It's done." Lois clicks on her phone and then puts it back in her pocket.

"We both appreciate it."

"It's not a problem. Please tell Kelly not to be shy about asking for what she needs here. The Glass House management and owners are friends to the Wolfe family, and we will accommodate Kelly in any way we can."

"Thank you."

Lois nods and whisks away from the table toward the break room.

But a minute later she's back, her face pale.

"Mr. Ramsey?"

"Yes? What is it?"

"Come with me please. It's Kelly."

My heart thrums as I rise, ready to face battle. I bolt to the back of the restaurant through the break room and into the women's room.

Kelly is lying in a fetal position, tears rolling out of her eyes.

The stench of vomit hangs in the air.

I go to her, lie down on the floor, cradle her against my body. "Kelly? Kelly, baby. What happened?"

She doesn't reply, just continues her silent sobbing.

"She's been sick," Lois says. "The sink is clogged with puke."

"I'm sorry."

"Oh, it's no problem. We've seen worse in our bathrooms. Custodial will be in soon and they'll take care of it."

"Kelly, can you come with me?" I ask softly.

Her tears continue to roll, but she nods.

"Good." I kiss her. Then I rise, hold out my hands for her.

She stretches her legs, but she still stays lying on the floor. So I kneel and help her into a sitting position.

"Lois has to have the bathrooms cleaned, Kelly. We need to leave."

She looks up. "Yeah."

I stand again, and this time she takes my hand and allows me to pull her up next to me. "Can you walk?"

"Yes."

"All right. Let's get you home."

She shakes her head then. "No. We have to call the police, Leif. We have to call the police."

I'm surprised at her statement, given her run-in with the police this morning. "Why? What happened?"

"He was here, Leif." She hiccups, her voice shaking. "The Dark One."

"The Dark One?"

"Mr. Smith. The one who sent me the texts. The letter. The man from the island. He was here."

Rage pulses through me.

It's an old feeling. One I know well. When Wolf died.

When that suicide bomber killed Buck's woman. When those motherfuckers came into my cell and did things to me that no one should ever have to endure.

Rage.

It starts in my stomach, in the pit of my gut. My internal organs clench together, hardening with blood. It flows outward, burning through my veins and up my spine until it bites the back of my neck, making me insane.

He was here?

In this bathroom? With the woman I love?

I gaze into her tired blue eyes, my own on fire. "What? Here? In this bathroom? With you?"

She nods, hiccupping again.

"Did you scream? My God, I'll never forgive myself if I didn't hear you scream."

She shakes her head. "I didn't. I couldn't."

"Did he hurt you?"

"No." She shakes her head again. "But he said he killed Brindley. And he said he'd be back."

"Kelly, what did he want?"

She pauses a moment, swallowing. Then, "Me."

"Over my fucking dead body," I say through clenched teeth. "Did he touch anything? Was he wearing gloves?"

"I... I don't know. All I saw was his hair, his eyes, his white mask, just like on the island. But he didn't touch anything. He didn't touch me."

"He must've touched the door to get into the bathroom. We'll have to have it dusted for prints."

Lois, who's been standing frozen until now, comes to life. "Right. I'm going to call the police right away. Right now."

"Do you have security cameras?" I ask.

"Yes, of course. But not in the break room or the bathrooms. I'll check with the kitchen. Maybe someone saw him come in." She leaves the bathroom, pulling her phone out of her pocket as she goes.

"Kelly, baby. Did he give you anything? Did he make you swallow anything? Is that why you got sick?"

"No. I threw up after he left. I... I just..."

I press two fingers over her lips. No need for her to explain. The encounter made her sick. The poor thing is exhausted, and the fright of seeing him... It's a wonder all she did was throw up.

And now I have to tell her that the police are coming, and we're going to have to stay here and talk to them.

Again.

"Come on, baby. Come out with me to the dining room. We'll sit at one of the booths where you can be comfortable." I lead her out of the bathroom and into the break room, and then I notice the couch lining one wall. "Better yet, I want you to lie down on the couch. That will be much more comfortable than a dining room table."

I take her to the couch, help her sit down, and she moves into a supine position, cradling her head on the arm of the couch.

I grab a pillow from one of the chairs. "Here, this will be more comfortable." I move her downward and ease the pillow under her neck. "Better?" I ask.

She nods but doesn't say anything.

Lois bustles back in the breakroom. "Cops are on their way, and the kitchen staff didn't notice anyone coming in the back way. Is she okay?"

"She'll be fine. She's strong."

"Goodness, she would have to be." Lois's chin trembles. "I'll wait outside for the police."

I brush my lips over Kelly's. "I love you. I love you so much."

She doesn't respond, not that I expect her to. How much trauma is one woman expected to live through?

If I could erase all of this, I would. Hell, I'd give my own life if I could erase all of the trauma from Kelly's past.

But I can't. No one can.

All I can do is love her and protect her with everything in me.

I'll do all of that, but I'm beginning to lose faith in my own abilities.

I sat in that restaurant in a central location for Kelly's entire shift. I had my eyes on the entrance every couple of minutes. I followed Kelly with my gaze, and I kept watch on the entry to the kitchen.

What did I miss?

How did that degenerate get into this restaurant? How did he get to Kelly?

I left her alone. I left her alone to go to the bathroom after her shift was over.

If I had insisted on accompanying her to the bathroom, she would've balked, and for good reason. But damn... Have I become lazy?

Who is this freak? And how does he appear from nowhere?

19

KELLY

And again, I'm answering questions.

I've become numb, robotic. I answer in one or two words, my tone monotonous.

Leif clasps my hand tightly through the whole thing.

"And you didn't see him enter the premises, sir?" a police officer asks Leif.

Leif tenses. I can feel it in his hand on mine.

"I did not."

"Yet you were in the restaurant during the whole shift for the sole purpose of keeping watch on Ms. Taylor?"

"Yes," he grits out.

"Very good." The officer turns to Lois. "I'm going to need you to show me all points of egress and ingress from this restaurant."

"Of course. Right away."

"Can I please go now?" I ask.

"Yes," the officer says. "You and Mr. Ramsey may leave. If I have further questions, I have your information and I'll be in touch."

Leif rises, glaring at the officer, and takes my hand. He doesn't say anything as he leads me out of the building, and we grab a cab back to the apartment.

He takes me directly to his place. "Do you need a shower?"

"God, I do," I tell him, "but I'm just too tired."

"All right." He takes my hand, leads me to the bedroom, helps me undress, and then puts me in bed, covering me. He kisses me on the forehead.

"Go to sleep. I'm going to case this apartment and make sure everything's fine."

I nod. Or I try to.

Worry consumes me, fear consumes me, rage consumes me... But I need sleep, and I succumb much quicker than I expect.

LEIF IS ABOVE ME, kissing me, making me feel loved and cherished.

He breaks the kiss, stares into my eyes, and then he enters me, slowly sliding into me, filling me.

I embrace the fullness, revel in it, love the feel of him completing me.

He looks in my eyes, gazes at me hypnotically, as he makes love to me slowly.

I close my eyes, enjoy the feeling of pure peace and completion that comes with making love with Leif.

Feelings I never thought I'd have.

Yes, I love you, Leif. I love you.

Dreamily, I open my eyes—

I jerk upward in bed.

Gasping.

"Leif!" I shout.

Seconds later, Leif stands in the doorway. "Kelly? What happened, baby?" He rushes to my side, puts his arms around me.

"I was... I was asleep, I think. I was..." My cheeks warm. "You and I. We were making love."

"That sounds like a good dream," he says.

"It was... I felt so good. So complete. But then—" I shudder.

"What, baby?"

"I had my eyes closed, and I felt so wonderful, until I opened my eyes and... It wasn't you anymore, Leif. It wasn't you."

He rubs circles into my back. "It's okay. I'm here now."

"Your eyes were blue. It was you before I closed my own. Then when I opened them... Your eyes were his, Leif. Dark brown, and—" I sob into him.

"Kelly, it was just a dream. A dream that turned into a nightmare. I'm so sorry. I should've stayed with you."

"No, no," I gulp. "It's more important that you make sure the apartment is secure. Is it?"

"Yes, so far. I've checked everything except in here, the bedroom."

"Okay. Please check it thoroughly."

"You can bet I will. I promise you that Mr. Smith is not getting in here. Not while I'm here."

I believe him. I believe Leif. But The Dark One got in the restaurant somehow. Of course, the restaurant has several doors, and Leif doesn't have eyes in the back of his head. This apartment only has one point of entry. No balcony or fire escape. Probably not the safest thing, but I understand why the Wolfes gave us only one point of entrance.

So that we—the victims of their father—would feel safe.

But I'm not safe. The Dark One knows where I live. He got into the building, found my apartment, and left me that scathing note. And then he found out where I work, got in there as well, and...

Images replay in my head, but I block them out. One thing all the years of my mother and all the years on the island did for me—I'm good at blocking things out.

I squeeze my eyes shut, burrowing my nose into Leif's shoulder.

"Kelly, I'm happy to stay here and hold you, but I can't do that if you want me to check the bedroom and bathroom."

He's right, of course. I pull back, gulping. "Yes. Please check the room. I'm so scared, Leif. How did he get into this building? How did he get into the restaurant?"

"I'm much more concerned about this building," Leif says. "The restaurant has several entrance points. The main one, of course, where customers and employees go in, but there are two in the back. One for deliveries and one for refuse pickup. Clearly he used one of those. I had one eye on the entrance at all times, even after the doors closed for the evening. I knew there were other points of entry, and I probably should've had them watched as well."

"I don't know how that would've helped," I say. "Three security guards on duty at the apartment, and he got past them. Have they found the two that are missing yet?"

"No, Kelly. They haven't."

I shiver. Falling in love with Leif has made me so much more aware of other people. Those two officers who are missing. Do they have families? Significant others? Children? People who are destroyed because they're missing?

The Dark One doesn't care about any of that. He cares only about himself. A classic narcissist, as Macy would say.

Leif touches my hair, kisses my cheek, and then he rises. He switches on the lights, and I squint against the glare, but my eyes quickly adjust. Leif checks the bedroom thoroughly. Exactly the way he checked my place a few days ago when I asked him to.

He's done in about half an hour, and then he strips off his clothes and gets into bed beside me.

He spoons me against his warm body, kissing my neck. "Go to sleep now, baby. I'm here, and no one can harm you."

His hard cock presses against my lower back, and I undulate my hips against him. I'm still wearing my underwear, but nothing else. He's completely naked.

"Please..." I say.

"You need to sleep."

"I'll sleep better if you do. Please." I push my panties down over my hips. Wriggle out of them quickly.

"If you're sure..." He kisses my neck and slides his dick between my ass cheeks, finding my pussy.

I warm, quaking in anticipation.

The head of his cock teases my pussy lips, and then—

I suck in a breath as he pushes inside me in one perfect thrust.

He groans against me. "God, Kelly. You feel so good."

"You do too. Take me away, Leif. Take me away from all this shit in the world."

"None of that exists right now. Only me. Only you. Only our love."

He slides in and out of me, and I undulate against him, meeting his thrusts. He slides his arm over my hips, and his fingers find my clit. He massages it slowly, methodically, in time with his thrusts, and soon my nipples are puckering, my pussy is throbbing, and I'm ready, ready, ready—

"God yes…" I say on a sigh.

The climax is different from the others. It's soft and sweet and full of protective wonder. He continues to glide in and out of me, the pressure on my clit lessening, and then he thrusts hard, growling.

As my climax subsides, he releases, and I relish every pulse of his cock inside me.

"God, baby. I guess we both needed that."

"Yes," I say on another sigh. "Yes. I think I can sleep now. But don't let go of me, Leif. Hold me all night long."

"You bet I will." He kisses my earlobe, slides his hand up, cupping one of my breasts.

I close my eyes, and I drift off.

This time…only Leif will be in my dreams.

20

LEIF

I wake early, which is normal for me no matter how much sleep I get. Some Navy habits are hard to break. It's a little after six a.m., and Kelly's still sleeping peacefully next to me.

I hold her close to me, trying to get back to sleep, but it's no use. I hate to leave her, but I crawl out of bed and try to be very quiet as I go into the bathroom and take a shower.

Once I'm done, I dress in jeans and a T-shirt, my hair still wet, and pad as quietly as I can to the kitchen where I start a pot of coffee.

I haven't yet told Kelly that she doesn't have to work tonight. Knowing her, she'll lash out at me for changing her schedule, but in the end she'll be grateful. She needs a day off. A day when she doesn't leave my side, when she doesn't need to be afraid of anything.

I have plenty of groceries in the apartment, and even though I'm not much of a cook, Kelly and I will have enough to eat today without leaving the apartment.

When she wakes up, if the two of us do nothing but make love all day, I won't have any complaints.

Once the coffee is brewed, I pour myself a cup and grab a couple of doughnuts out of the breadbox. Then I sit down at my small table, open my iPad, and read the news for the day.

Nothing about the break-in at the building, and nothing about what happened at the restaurant last night. Good.

The Wolfes do as much as they can to keep their father's victims out of the press. I'm sure a lot of reporters have been paid a handsome paycheck for not printing stories.

The last thing Kelly needs is to see her name plastered across some tabloid.

I check my emails, check in with Reid, and once eight o'clock rolls around, I go into the bedroom to make sure Kelly is okay.

She's sitting up in bed, stretching her arms.

"Hey, sleepyhead," I say. "I was hoping you'd still be asleep. You need your rest."

"No," she says. "It's better if I keep regular hours."

"Regular hours for you, with your evening shift, means sleeping until ten or eleven, Kelly."

"I can't do that. I've tried. I'll just have to learn to get by on less sleep." She tosses the covers off. "Actually, I don't even have to learn. I'm doing it."

"I have good news for you."

She widens her eyes. "They found him?"

"Well, not that good of news. But you don't have to work tonight."

She raises an eyebrow. "What do you mean I don't have to work tonight? I'm scheduled."

"Lois changed you to Sunday," I say.

"Why? And why would she do that without telling me? What if I'm busy on Sunday?"

"Are you?"

She frowns. "Well... No, but—"

I quiet her with two fingers on her soft lips. "No buts, Kelly. It was Lois's idea, and it was a good one. She knows what you've been through. She knows how late we were talking to police officers last night because she was there as well."

Kelly opens her mouth—to object, I'm sure—but then closes it.

"Good. You've decided not to fight me."

"Would it do me any good?"

"Absolutely not. You know as well as I do that this is what's best for you. You've worked two shifts at The Glass House so far, and you've kicked ass on both, including last night when you were working on empty. You need to take today. We're not leaving this place. I have food, and I'm going to cook for you."

"You know how to cook?"

"Not exactly, but Reid left me a cookbook."

"God... Well, it just so happens that I *do* know how to cook. I worked in a diner for five years, remember?"

"As a server, not a cook."

"But I—" She clamps her mouth shut.

"What?"

She bites her lip. "I cooked a lot when I was a kid. I was expected to make dinner for my mom from the time I was about eight years old. And believe me, I had to get really creative because there was never much food in our house."

"Kelly..."

She shakes her head vehemently. "I don't want your pity, Leif. Not now, and not ever."

"Honey, it's not pity. It's concern. It's sadness. Aren't I allowed to feel bad about what you went through?"

"No."

"Sorry. You're not in charge of my feelings, Kelly. Just like I'm not in charge of yours."

She opens her mouth again but shuts it.

"I'm happy to cook. If you want to, I will gladly give it up."

She sighs. "I need a shower."

"All right. I'll give you some privacy."

"Who said I wanted any privacy?"

"I was trying to be a gentleman, Kelly."

"I know, but..."

"But what?"

"It's just... This is going to sound ridiculous, but I'm not used to gentlemen, Leif. I'm used to men taking what they want from me."

My heart cracks. Every time I hear another story about her life, about how she was treated, about how she never knew how worthy she was...I lose a little bit more of that vital organ.

"I'll never do that," I say. "I swear to God, Kelly."

"I know."

"That's not what you want, is it?"

She shakes her head. "No. It's never what I wanted. I just... Never mind."

"I understand. I knew some people from my time overseas who had bad cases of Stockholm syndrome. I'm glad that's not you."

"Are you kidding me? I don't want The Dark One coming after me. I hate him. How did he find me?"

"I don't know, my love, but he won't come near you again."

"Promise?"

"I promise." I kiss her lips and hope to God I'm not lying to her. I rise and help her to her feet.

"About that shower..." She licks her bottom lip.

My cock is straining. She's naked and so beautiful, I have to give her what she wants.

"All right, Kelly. But please say you'll respect me afterward." I smile as I pull my T-shirt over my head.

She sucks in a breath as she gazes at my chest.

I feel like puffing myself out like a peacock, but I resist. I know how attractive she finds me. Almost as attractive as I find her. She's freaking luscious.

"I need to brush my teeth." She makes a face. "I should've done it last night."

"The bathroom's yours. Brush your teeth and then start the shower. I'll be there in five minutes."

She nods and pads to the shower as I watch her delectable ass and long legs.

I hear her turn on the faucet, and then I kick off my slippers and quickly remove my jeans and underwear.

My cock is already hard and ready.

I give her time to take care of things, and then walk to the bathroom once I hear the water running for the shower.

You can never have too many showers—especially when a beautiful woman is in there with you.

Kelly steps into the shower, and I follow her. She closes her eyes, lets the water flow over her hair, pasting it back.

I can't help myself. I reach forward and tweak both her

nipples, and then twist them between my thumb and forefingers. She gasps slightly and opens her eyes, floating into my arms. I hoist her against my chest, move her against the shower wall, and then thrust my cock up into her.

Already I know I won't last long, and already she's writhing with me, her legs clamped around me, her fingers threading through my hair.

"Yes, Leif. Please... Please..."

I know what she wants. She's not interested in an orgasm. She's interested in a fucking. A good cleansing fucking. I understand.

And I'm very willing to do my part.

I thrust, and I thrust, and I thrust, and already I pump my seed into her.

We're not using condoms anymore, and her pussy feels like it was made specifically for my cock. So tight, full of ridges, and the warmth and suction drives me mad.

Once my climax subsides, she slides off me, placing her feet back on the wet shower floor.

"Thank you," she says.

"Baby, you don't ever have to thank me for that."

"But I do," she says. "It's important for me to thank you, Leif."

I narrow my gaze. "Why? I mean I understand why you'd want to thank me for something else, but for fucking you in the shower? You didn't even come, Kelly."

"Because it's what I needed and wanted," she says. "This is kind of amazing to me, Leif. I haven't said thank you a lot in my life because I haven't had a lot to be thankful for. I was thankful when a customer used to leave me a big tip at the diner, but by the time I usually found out about the tip, the customer was long gone, so I couldn't say thank you. Everyone else? There was just no reason to say thank you. I was just living a life, and the life was... Well, it was a hell of a lot better than my childhood with my mother, but I guess I never learned to be grateful. Even on the island, I was never grateful on those nights I didn't get chosen. I look back at all of that now, and it seems so foreign to me."

"I'm glad it seems foreign." I grab my shampoo bottle and squeeze some into my palm. Then I squeeze a little more, because Kelly's hair is a lot longer than mine. I lather it in my hands and then place my hands on her head, massaging it gently into her scalp. "I understand what you mean, though. There were times when I was overseas in Afghanistan when it was hard to find anything to be thankful for. But I learned that as long as my heart was beating and my lungs were breathing, I had a lot to be thankful for. Some of my buddies no longer have that."

She bites on her lip.

"What is it?" I ask.

She looks down at her feet. "I feel so...ridiculous some-times when you talk about your time overseas."

"Why?"

"Because you're such a good man, Leif. You served your country. You saved a fallen man."

"I saved several. But I also let several die, and I have to live with that every day. No one is a true hero, Kelly. But I'm glad you think I'm a good man."

"I do." She meets my gaze but then looks down. "I don't think anyone has ever thought of me as a good person."

"I do. Do you think I could fall in love with a bad person?"

"I'm... I'm afraid you might have."

I turn around so that she's facing the water. "Close your eyes while I rinse your hair."

She bows her head, and as the water drizzles through her hair, I rinse the shampoo from her, watching the suds swirl down the drain. Once her hair is squeaky clean, I turn her back around, place her head under the shower so her hair is now out of her face. Then I cup both her cheeks. "You listen to me, and you listen good. There is no black-and-white in this world. Everything is shades of gray. There's no absolute good and absolute bad."

"Oh, there's absolute bad."

I pause. "Yeah, that's a hard one for me to swallow too. But when Buck and I got back from that last tour, we were discharged honorably, and we both had a lot of PTSD. We went to therapy together and solo for a while. One thing I learned was that even those who appear to be nothing but pure evil usually have one tiny redeeming quality. It's just very hard to find, and no one usually sees it."

"I don't think The Dark One has any redeeming qualities," she says with a scoff, "and I can't believe you would say that he does." She turns from me then, opens the shower door, and gets out, dripping onto the bathmat as she grabs a towel.

"Kelly, I—"

She slams the door to the bathroom.

I suppose I deserve that. Probably wasn't the best time to bring up that little tidbit from my therapy. To be honest, I don't always believe it either, but for the most part, I believe that there are no absolutes in life. It took me a long time to realize it, but the people who tortured me while I was in captivity were either following orders or they were doing what they thought was best for their country. Or there was a different motive. Perhaps their loved ones were being threatened. Or perhaps there was a reason I can't even fathom. But there was a motive, nonetheless. That didn't mean it was a good motive.

But...Kelly's experience was completely different. Men paid millions to subject her to the abuse and torture on that island. Their motive? Their own warped and narcissistic pleasure.

She's right.

There was no good in any of them.

A year of therapy down the drain. Sometimes, there is an absolute, and this Dark One who is bent on tormenting Kelly is absolute evil.

I don't bother washing my hair. Just my private parts, as I've already had a shower today. I get out, dry myself off, and wrap a towel around my waist. I open the door. Kelly's already gone. She clearly put her clothes from last night back on.

She must be out in the kitchen, maybe getting something to eat.

I put on my clothes, towel off my hair, and head back out.

"Kelly? Kelly, I'm sorry. You're right."

She's not in the kitchen. And she's not at the table drinking coffee... And she's not—

"Kelly!"

She probably just went back to her place. No reason to get freaked out.

I leave my apartment, and I don't even bother knocking on her door. I slide my key through and open it. "Kelly?"

I expect to see her sitting on her couch, or in the kitchen getting some coffee together.

She's in neither of those places, and my heart starts to explode.

I walk to her bedroom—the door is closed. I knock. "Kelly? I'm sorry, baby. I shouldn't have said that kind of stuff."

I turn the knob and open the door. "Kelly?"

She's not in the bedroom. I check the bathroom quickly, my pulse on overload. Then I check her walk-in closet.

"Kelly!"

My nerves are jumping, and my heart is pounding so hard I can actually see the movement against my chest.

"Kelly!" I grab fists of my hair. "Kelly, where the fuck are you?"

21

KELLY

"Yes? Come in," Macy says after I pound on her door on the first floor of the building.

I open the door and poke my head in.

"Kelly," she says, smiling. "What can I do for you?"

"I need to talk to you. I know it's not my regular session, but do you have ten minutes?"

"Of course." She gestures. "Come on in and sit down."

I close the door and take a seat in my usual chair across from her desk.

"I'm not surprised to see you, given what you've been through."

"You don't know the half of it."

"There hasn't been any news on those two security guards from the other night, I'm afraid," she says.

Now I feel like a self-centered piece of crap. I haven't even been thinking about them because I'm so angry with Leif right now.

"I'm so sorry to hear that," I say.

"Me too. I knew one of them quite well. He was young,

newly engaged." She shakes her head. "But unfortunately there's nothing we can do about that except pray. What can I do for you today?"

"You can tell me," I say, "whether there's truly good in everyone."

"Well," she sighs. "I'm glad you didn't ask me an easy question. Maybe you'd rather know something simple, like whether there's a God, or what is the meaning of the universe?"

I know she's trying to be funny, but my question is valid.

"I'm serious. I think…"

"You think what?"

"I don't know. I'm just really angry with Leif. He gave me some gobbledygook about how he came home from the conflict in Afghanistan, how he had PTSD and went to therapy, and one of the things he learned was that there were no absolutes. No absolute good or absolute evil."

"I can see why that upset you."

"Thank you. Because clearly he didn't see it at all. My mother for example. Absolute evil. This degenerate who's chasing me around Manhattan right now. Absolute evil."

"It would seem that way, on the surface."

"On the surface? My God, you're going to say the same thing, aren't you?"

"No. I'm not going to say the same thing. I'm going to say that perhaps it helped Leif in his healing to feel that there were no absolutes. It may have nothing to do with good and evil. It could mean an absolute of another kind."

"What other kind?"

"The world is full of shades of gray, Kelly. My guess is that when Leif had that eye-opening epiphany during his therapy, it had to do with something completely different from what you're dealing with."

"Or maybe..." I shake my head, closing my eyes. "No, I can't imagine that. Not Leif. Not someone so strong and virile and courageous."

"Where is your mind going?" Macy asks.

"To dark places. Places I don't want to think about."

"All right. You just say what you feel you can say."

"He's so strong. So muscular, I mean, if you could see him." My cheeks warm.

"I've seen him, Kelly. He's tall and muscular, yes. Very handsome."

A twinge of jealousy gets me then.

Macy is no threat. I know that I'm just reacting the way I've been reacting my whole life.

"Do you think... I mean, military activities..." I shake my head. "I don't know what I'm saying. I'm sorry to bother you." I rise.

"Please, sit back down. I have the time, and this is clearly important to you."

I obey her, sitting down.

"I think what you're imagining, what you're wondering, is whether something as horrific as what happened to you might have happened to Leif."

I close my eyes and nod.

I'm glad she said the words because I just couldn't.

"The only person who can answer that question is Leif," she says, "and if something terrible did happen, he may not want to talk about it."

"I know. It took me a long time to talk about...everything."

"I know it did, but you've done wonderfully. Look at Leif

now. He's an incredible person, and whatever happened to him, he's worked through it."

I nod.

"And if it helped him to imagine that someone who may have tortured him in some way had a smidgen of good in them, who are we to question that?"

"But how can he? I mean, was there a smidgen of good in Hitler? In Osama bin Laden? In Jeffrey Dahmer?"

"I don't know," Macy says. "I'm not sure if we're meant to know those kinds of things."

I draw in a breath, mentally counting to ten. "I will never believe it, Macy. I will never believe that there was one tiny microscopic particle of good in any of the men on that island, or in my mother, and especially not in this Mr. Smith who is still out there and still wants to violate me."

"I will never ask you to believe that."

"Good. Because I won't. I can't believe that Leif does."

"Don't hold Leif's views against him," Macy says. "Neither one of us knows what he's been through."

"I..." I shake my head again, trying to erase the images that want to erupt. Images of Leif... Being hurt. Tortured.

"Why did I start going down this path?" I ask. "Now, I think... My God, Leif..."

Macy reaches across her desk and pats my hand. "Leif is fine, Kelly. Whatever he's been through, he's worked through it. That much is clear. And whatever he's doing, whatever he says to you, I feel certain that his end goal is to help you. Certainly not to hurt you. Nor to anger you."

I don't reply.

"You've come so far on your anger," Macy says. "Don't

forget the progress you've made just because someone close to you said something you disagree with."

"That's it, isn't it? It's because I love Leif. And because he loves me. And I expect him to…"

"You expect him to agree with you on everything. I'm pretty sure he does agree that what you've been through is heinous. What those men did to you and the other girls is unforgivable. And what you're going through now is frightening. All he wants to do is protect you and help you in any way he can. If he falls back on something that helped him, give him a little slack. Perhaps it's not something that will help you, but he doesn't know that. He's doing the best he can, same as we all are."

I breathe in again, count to ten again.

Then I open my eyes. Macy is looking at me sternly. She has never steered me wrong, and I have no reason to believe she's steering me wrong now.

I rise. "All right, Macy. Thank you for seeing me without an appointment."

"Anytime I'm here and not with another patient, you are welcome to come. You know that."

"Yeah, I do. And please, let me know if you find out anything about the two security guards who are missing."

Macy smiles. "You're making progress, Kelly. You realize that this is the first time I've actually heard you express concern over another person?"

I open my mouth, but nothing comes out. Seriously? Have I been that shortsighted, that self-absorbed all this time?

"Brindley…" I say on a sigh.

"I know, sweetheart. I'll miss her too."

"I treated her so badly."

"Yes, but as I understand it, in the end, the two of you patched things up."

"I suppose we did, but how can mere words make up for the way I acted?"

"Words go a long way, but of course actions speak louder."

"But I can't use my actions now. She's gone."

"Yes, she's gone, but take solace in the fact that wherever she is now, she knows for sure how much you regret your actions. And use this as a learning tool."

In other words, don't treat people so horribly from now on. That's what Macy wants to say, but she's a genius at being diplomatic.

I nod. "Thanks again, Macy. I guess I'll see you tomorrow at my regular session."

"I'll be here."

I nod, leave, closing the door behind me.

Only to drop my jaw.

22

LEIF

I grab her like a madman. Shake her. "Don't you ever do that to me again!"

"Do what? I had to talk to Macy."

"You should've told me. I would've come with you. You are *not* to leave the apartment without me, do you understand?"

She lifts her chin defiantly. "No, Leif. I don't understand. You're not the boss of me. No one controls me. I've taken care of myself for—"

Anger spurs in me, anger fueled by the relief, by her admission that she left without telling me.

I raise my hand, and she winces.

I look at my hand and then back at her. "Afraid of me, Kelly? Do you really think, after all we've been through, that I would dare to strike you?"

"Why did you raise your hand?"

"Because I'm angry. Because I'm ready to put my fist through a wall. But I would never, ever put my fist through you, Kelly. I would never harm a hair on your sweet head."

She pulls away from my grip and I let go.

"Don't do it again," I say. "I can't protect you if I don't know where you are."

"Give me a little bit of credit, Leif. I've got a psychopath after me. Do you really think I would leave the security of this building?"

"I think it's been proven that this building is *not* secure when it comes to the psychopath who is after you."

"I think it's also been proven that I'm not secure when you're around." Her tone reeks of venom as she crosses her arms over her chest. "The psychopath got into the restaurant, got to me last night."

Oh God…

I know I should count to ten, but I don't.

"That's hitting below the belt," I grit out, "and you fucking know it."

"How is it—"

"We were in a public place. A fucking restaurant, Kelly. Not a building with security. And yes, he breached this building the other night, but you remained safe, didn't you? You remained safe because you were locked in my apartment. My apartment that I checked thoroughly for any kind of security breach."

I breathe in, breathe out.

"Well, I—"

I don't hear. I grab her arm and yank her to the elevators. "You're coming up to the apartment with me, and you're not leaving. Not until we find that psycho and stop him."

She opens her mouth again, but nothing comes out.

Good. Maybe she's learned her lesson.

She stops fighting me and walks willingly with me to the elevator, where I push the button for the fourth floor.

"Why don't these elevators have key cards?" she asks. "Why don't the stairwells have key cards to open? Turns out this building is not as secure as the mighty Wolfe family thinks."

I say nothing.

I say nothing because Kelly is right. No doubt Reid and the Wolfes felt that the first floor security was sufficient. Guards outside the door. Guards outside the back doors as well. Keyed entry, and security at a desk.

But it's not sufficient. The Dark One, as Kelly refers to him, clearly got through. And the two guards are still missing.

"Don't you have anything to say?" she asks haughtily.

"No, Kelly. I have nothing more to say to you."

We reach the fourth floor, and she stops at the door to her place.

"Nope." I say. "You're staying in my apartment."

She sets her hands on her hips. "I'd rather have my finger-nails pulled off."

"I'm sure we can arrange that," I say dryly.

"Who the hell do you think you are?" Her voice brims with acid.

"I'm the man who loves you, though you make me rethink that every day. I'm the man hired to keep you safe. And damn it, that is what I intend to do."

I walk to the door of my apartment, slide the key card through, and to my surprise, Kelly walks in ahead of me.

Apparently I won this battle.

But the war is far from over.

What will it take? I love her, and I know she loves me. But

what will it take for her to get rid of the last of the venom she still holds inside her?

It took a while for me to get over the PTSD from my tours, but there's one huge difference between Kelly and me.

I entered the Navy of my own free will. I chose to serve my country, and when I went on each of my tours, I knew all the risks. I knew that it wouldn't all be pretty. I knew that it could be downright ugly, downright torturous. And some of it was.

But still, I entered into that contract with my country willingly.

Kelly did not enter into her life willingly. She didn't sign up for a mother who abused her and neglected her and locked her in a closet. She didn't sign up for five years on that horrific island.

No. All of that was thrust upon her without her consent.

I need to remember that.

I soften. "You frightened me, Kelly. When I got out of the shower, and I couldn't find you, I –" I close my eyes and shake my head.

Is it time to truly reveal myself to her? She knows my feelings, but does she know how a dagger pierced my heart when I thought she might be gone?

"Please, Kelly. I'm trying to be understanding. If you love me, you—"

"No," she says. "I do love you, Leif. But I'm not going to put any conditions on that love. So don't give me any of that 'if you love me' bullshit. I *do* love you."

"Then may I ask *why* you frightened me?"

"I was angry."

"So you're admitting you knew I'd be frightened when I found you gone."

She bites on her lip.

Yeah, she knew.

"Look, love is beautiful. It's amazing, but it's also about respect, Kelly. It's about respect in spite of anger. And when you respect someone, you don't deliberately frighten them."

Her eyelids flutter and she looks to the floor.

I don't say anything more.

About a moment later, she looks up. "You're right, Leif. I apologize."

Thank God.

She's not regressing after all. She just reverted to her old ways in a fit of anger. Hell, I've done that more than once.

My phone buzzes in the back of my pocket.

God, great timing, this. But I have to check. It could be important.

And it is.

It's Reid Wolfe.

"Yeah?" I say into the phone.

"Did I catch you at a bad time?" he asks.

"Yeah, you did. What can I do for you, Reid?"

"I'd say it can wait, but it can't. Racine Taylor has been in contact with Rock and me again. She's still adamant about seeing Kelly."

"I told her Kelly doesn't want to see her."

Kelly's eyes widen at her name.

"Well," Reid says, "we certainly won't force her to. But Racine says it's important."

"If there was anything that important, she could've disclosed it to me the other night when I met with her."

Reid clears his throat. "She says this is new. Information she didn't have at that time."

"For Christ's sake. I don't know what the woman wants, but it's clear she has no feelings for her daughter. She's got all the money she could want, so what the hell is she after?"

"She may have a lot of money," Reid says, "but I have a lot more. Some people get a taste of money, and then however much they have is never enough."

"Kelly doesn't have any," I say.

Again Kelly raises her eyebrows.

"No, but I do. And Racine no doubt knows that my family will do anything for these women."

"What do you want me to do?"

"I've invited Racine to meet with us tomorrow morning, Nine a.m. in the same conference room at the office. I'd like you to be there."

"I'm happy to be there, but I won't leave Kelly alone. Not with what's going on."

"Not a problem. I'll send someone else to stay with her."

"No offense, Reid, but the only other person I trust is Buck, and he's out of town."

"Now wait just a minute—"

"Don't take it the wrong way," I say, "but two of your security guards are still missing."

He says nothing. What can he say anyway? My words are fact.

Finally, "All right. If you can't be there, I'll set up a conference call."

"I will come if Kelly consents to come with me, but I doubt she will."

I'm not thrilled about the idea of Kelly leaving the building, especially not after what happened last night at the restaurant, but this will be different. She won't leave my side.

"Good enough. You let me know which way it's going to be by eight in the morning."

"Will do. See you, Reid."

Kelly doesn't wait long to pounce after I end the call.

"I really don't like you talking about me."

"It was just Reid."

"What's going on with my mother?"

"She says she has some information that she didn't give me the other night."

"I don't care what information she may have."

"Truthfully, neither do I, but she's somehow convinced Reid and Rock to meet with her. They would like the two of us to be there."

"I won't see her," she harrumphs.

"I understand. And I won't leave you, so that means we'll set it up as a conference call at my apartment."

"Then I don't want to be in your apartment during that time."

"Kelly, can you for once not be so difficult?"

I berate myself for the words as soon as I say them. Of course she's difficult. She's been through hell not only her whole life but the last two days as well, when the Wolfes promised to keep her safe.

When *I* promised to keep her safe.

"I'm sorry," I say softly. "That was out of line."

She shakes her head. "No, you weren't out of line, Leif." She smirks. "Well, maybe you were, but so was I."

I can't help smiling, and I trail a finger over her soft cheek.

149

Just when I think she's reverted to her venomous ways, she surprises me yet again.

Kelly really is a beautiful and loving soul. But that beautiful, loving soul has never been nurtured, not by her mother, and not by anyone else.

"Kelly?"

"Yeah?"

"Did you ever look for your father? Once you left home?"

"No. Where would I begin? I pulled my birth certificate one time. My mother is listed as Racine Marie Taylor. The father is left blank."

"I see."

"So I have no idea."

I clear my throat. "I asked your mother about him."

"And? Did she lock you in the closet?"

"No." I let out a chuckle, though Kelly's comment is far from funny. "She just said he was never in the picture and that she doesn't speak of him."

"Yeah, exactly. I carry her last name, so I have no idea even where to start looking. I've considered getting one of those DNA kits that tell you your ethnic origins, and then they hook you up with any relative you might have—but I never did."

"Do you want to?"

"I don't know. What if he's some horrible derelict?"

"What if he's a millionaire?"

Kelly huffs. "If he were a millionaire, my mother would've never let him go that easily."

"When you're right, you're right." I sigh. "Well, it's up to you. I'd be happy to get you one of those kits if you want to look into it further. I'm sure the Wolfes could expedite the results for you."

"Is there anything they can't get by waving their money around?"

I smile at her then, cup her cheeks. "There's a lot of things their money can't do, Kelly. It hasn't protected you very well, and neither have I. But that's going to change."

"I don't blame any of this on you."

"I do."

"You kept me safe that first night, Leif. When he somehow got into the building."

"But I didn't keep you safe last night." I run my hand over my face. "I thank God you're okay, and I'm so sorry you had to deal with him."

"If you had it your way, you would've gone into the bathroom with me." She shakes her head. "I know you didn't want me working last night. And now...I'm beginning to think maybe I should take a leave of absence from the job until this is settled."

An anvil falls from my shoulders. "Are you serious, baby? I'm sure Linda and Lois will hire you right back when things get better."

"Even if they don't"—she shrugs—"I'll get another job. Maybe a better one."

"Thank God." I yank her to me. "Thank you. Now I can keep you with me, keep you safe."

"And I've been thinking..."

"About what?" I say into her hair.

"I think... I think I'll go with you tomorrow. To the office. To see my mother."

23

KELLY

I'm tense as I sit next to Leif. The conference room is the same as I remember—with Roy Wolfe's paintings on the wall. I stare at the three paintings, all abstract. Funny, they look completely different from the last time I saw them. The colors seem brighter, more vibrant.

Maybe that's what abstract art is all about.

We arrived early on purpose.

It was Leif's idea, and I agreed. If I'm here before my mother, I have the upper hand. I took ownership of this room before she got here. She cannot harm me.

Objectively, I know she can't harm me anyway. She has no power over me anymore.

Still...the scars run deep. She is my mother, and as her child, apparently I have a subconscious need to recognize her as an authority. Macy and I have talked about that before, and I would've had another talk about it with her today, except I had to reschedule my appointment this morning so I could come with Leif to this meeting.

This meeting with my mother.

Rock and Reid Wolfe sit at their respective places at either end of the table. Lacey sits next to Rock, across from me.

She smiles. "How are you doing, Kelly?"

How the hell does she think I'm doing?

But I hold back the venom. "As well as I can be, I suppose."

"I've been in touch with the detective who questioned you the other day," Lacey says. "She offered profuse apologies when she found out you were assaulted by your stalker at the restaurant last night."

"How nice of her." I roll my eyes.

"Yes. I suggested that she contact you and apologize to you personally, though I doubt she will. I have the utmost respect for all law enforcement officers, but it's been my experience that some of them have trouble admitting when they're wrong."

I say nothing more.

Then I jump out of my seat at a knock on the door.

"Come in," Rock says in his deep and gravelly voice.

A young woman—I haven't seen her before at the office—opens it. "Mr. Wolfe, Racine Taylor is here."

"Come on in then," Rock says.

Intentionally, I drop my gaze to the table. Though I yearn to look at her—to see what she looks like now—I force myself not to. No way will she think that I want to see her.

"Good morning, Ms. Taylor," Rock says as he rises. "I'm Rock Wolfe. This is my wife, Lacey, my brother Reid, Leif Ramsey, part of our security team, and of course you know your daughter."

"Kelly!" She rushes to me, wraps her arms around the

backs of my shoulders, and plants a wet kiss on my cheek. "Thank God you're all right."

"Like you care," I say.

"I've been trying to see you. Thank you so much for coming today."

I keep my gaze fixed on the table. "I didn't come for you. I came because Leif asked me to."

"Well, whatever the reason, it's so good to see you. You're looking as beautiful as ever."

I allow myself to look at my mother then. Even meet her gaze. Same blue eyes, same Lucille Ball red hair. She's put on a few pounds but still has a decent body for a woman her age. It's her clothing that draws my attention more than anything. Zebra-striped leggings and a black spandex shirt. Platform sandals. And red lips.

God, I probably have a kiss mark on my cheek.

"Ms. Taylor." Reid holds out a chair next to him. "Please, have a seat."

Mom sits down without a fuss and then gestures to the young woman who ushered her in. "Darling, I would love a coffee."

"Cream?" The woman asks.

"Only if it's Irish."

The young woman wrinkles her forehead.

"Cream and sugar, darling. That's fine for now." Mom bats her eyes.

"Yes. Right away." The woman disappears.

My cup of black coffee sits in front of me. I take a sip. It's good. Whoever makes the coffee here knows how to make it well.

"Ms. Taylor," Reid says, "you said you have some new

information for us. Information that you did not give to Mr. Ramsey the other night."

"Yes, yes, I do. You'll never guess who reached out to me, seemingly from nowhere."

"I couldn't venture to guess," Rock says dryly, clearly resisting an eyeroll.

My mother looks my way and smiles. "It was your father, Kelly. Can you believe it? After all these years?"

"Yeah, I don't believe it," I say. "You wouldn't even tell me his name."

"To be honest. I never knew his name. His last name, that is. I met him at a masquerade, and we had—well, you know what we did. You were the result."

"You've got to be kidding me," Leif says under his breath.

"Anyway," my mother continues, "he contacted me. Of course I didn't know him from Adam. But he knew exactly where I was that night, and although he was masked, I'll never forget those dark brown eyes of his."

"You mean he wasn't a redhead?" Leif asks.

"Heavens, no."

"Then where exactly did Kelly get the red hair?"

"Goodness, I'm not a geneticist," Racine says.

"Whoever contacted you was not my father," I say.

"Well of course he is," Racine says. "Like I said, I remember his eyes. And he had answers to questions only he would know."

"Then where did my red hair come from?" I ask. "Because we all know that yours is not red."

"Like I said, I'm not a geneticist."

Leif pulls his phone out, start tapping on it. "This is interesting."

"What is?" I ask.

"Apparently two parents who do not have red hair can have a redhaired child, if they both carry the redhaired gene."

"See? There. You see I'm not lying." Racine smiles.

"So what?" I say. "So maybe it was my father. Who cares?"

"The good news, darling, is that he's *rich*."

"So are you, apparently," I say dryly. "Not that you ever offered me a cent of your money."

"Darling, I never knew where you were. And then, when I found you, you refused to see me."

I roll my eyes, shaking my head.

"But your father has more money than I could ever dream of having on my own. Not just millions. *Billions*."

"Somehow I just can't believe you," I say.

"What's his name, Ms. Taylor?" Reid asks. "We need his name."

"Well, I didn't even know until now. But his name is Smith. Forrester Smith."

24

LEIF

Kelly goes rigid.

"Baby," I whisper to her, "it's not the same guy."

"She said dark eyes," she says.

I push my chair back. "Rock, Reid, you know all the billionaires. Have you ever heard of Forrester Smith?"

"Can't say that I have." Reid says.

"Me neither," Rock says gruffly.

"All I can tell you is what he told me," Racine says. "It's not like I asked to see his asset statements."

"We'll check him out, Ms. Taylor," Reid says.

"Thank you. Thank you very much." She leans toward Kelly. "In the meantime, he'd like to see you, Kelly."

"Wait, wait, wait," I say. "Something doesn't gel here. This guy just happens to come to you after all these years? Doesn't that seem a little too convenient?"

"I agree," Rock says.

"He reached out to me," Racine says. "That's all I can tell you. I didn't believe him at first either. When I met up with

157

him, I recognized his eyes, and like I said, he had answers to questions only he could know."

"When exactly did he reach out to you?" Reid asks.

"During my stay here in New York, actually. He left a message for me at my hotel, and we met up in the bar for a drink. I was as astonished as the rest of you are, I assure you. Like I said, I never knew his name."

"Why would he even think to reach out to you?" I ask. "Did he know your name? Did he somehow know he had fathered a child?"

"Your guess is as good as mine," Racine says.

"You mean you didn't ask him?" I ask.

"Of course she didn't ask him," Kelly says. "As soon as she heard about the billions of dollars, she didn't really care about the details."

Racine blushes a little. "Kelly, of course not."

"Yeah? Then why *didn't* you ask him? Why didn't you ask him how he knew he had fathered a child?"

"Well, perhaps he didn't know. He didn't bring it up. I did."

"And all of a sudden," I say, "this billionaire comes out of the woodwork, this billionaire you had a one-night stand with nearly thirty years ago, and you just buy it all?"

"I'm sorry," Racine says, "but I don't see what the big issue is here. This man is offering Kelly and me his fortune. We'd be stupid not to take it."

"Wait a minute..." I narrow my eyes at her. "He wants to give it to *both* of you, doesn't he? And he won't give it to you without Kelly."

She reddens further. "My goodness, do you think I'd really use my own daughter that way?"

What happens next surprises the hell out of me.

Kelly erupts into laughter. Maniacal laughter almost.

When she finally gets ahold of herself, she says, "Wow. I haven't laughed like that in a long time. Maybe ever. Thank you for that, Mom. I didn't think there'd ever be anything in the world that I would want to thank you for, but that? It felt good."

Racine rises. "Well, if you don't want the money, Kelly, I suppose I should leave."

"Do you have contact information for this man?" Reid asks.

"I do." Racine opens her purse, takes out a business card, and hands it to Reid. "He can be reached here."

Reid raises an eyebrow. "Uh...Ms. Taylor?"

"Yes?"

"You do realize this card says that he's a Starbucks barista?"

"Of course I realize that." Racine looks at her manicured fingernails. "You don't think a billionaire can just go handing out business cards, do you?"

Reid reaches into his pocket, pulls out his wallet, extracts a card. "Here's mine." He hands it to her.

I've seen Reid's business card, and nowhere does the word Starbucks appear.

"There's something really fishy about this," I say. "We'll look into it."

Kelly is still gulping back the end of her laughter. "You can bet it's fishy. Whoever that guy is, Mother, he's not my father. I mean, maybe you and my father both carry the redhaired gene, but it's much more likely that my father had red hair."

"I would never sleep with a redhead," Racine says.

"Then why do you dye your hair that god-awful color?" Rock asks.

"Rock!" Lacey admonishes.

Rock raises his hands in the air, clearly exasperated. "Well, for God's sake. This is all just a bunch of ridiculous bullshit. Anyone can see it. Anyone with a nose can sniff it out. Ms. Taylor, if you're looking for a handout from us, you're not going to get it."

"Do I look like I need a handout?" She waves her hand, gesturing to her diamond-studded watch. "I'm sure you've had me checked out. You know how much money I have."

Rock scoffs. "You just admitted that you want this man's billions."

"Of course I want his billions. He's Kelly's father. I raised her alone. I had no financial help at all. He owes me."

"So he owes you..." I say, "but what about Kelly?"

"Oh, of course." Racine attempts to save face. "He owes Kelly, too."

"We will check it out, Ms. Taylor," Reid says, glaring at Rock.

Rock just chuckles and shakes his head.

I rise then. "I'll see you out."

"Isn't that nice of you," Racine says.

"As long as the two of you remain in here with Kelly and ensure her safety," I say, glancing at Rock and Reid.

"Absolutely," Reid says. "You've got it."

Kelly looks at me, and I can't quite read her expression, but one thing is evident. She's not pleased.

"I'll explain later," I whisper to her and kiss her on the cheek.

Then I escort Racine out of the conference room and down the hall to the reception area.

"I saw you kiss my daughter," she says.

"So what?"

"What do you think—"

"Enough," I interrupt her. "Let's step outside in the hallway, and you and I will have a little chat." I lead her through the glass doors and then toward the elevators. "Get real with me now, Racine. None of this is true, is it?"

She blinks. "On the contrary, Leif. It's all true. The man reached out to me. Surprised me as much as anyone."

"How did he know you were here in the city?"

"I don't know."

"You didn't ask?"

"I guess I didn't think to."

I roll my eyes. "No, all you saw were dollar signs. How much money will be enough for you, Racine? You were paid off five years ago—"

"What are you talking about?"

"Oh, save it. I know you received payments totaling two million dollars starting six months after Kelly was abducted. Did you even *know* she was abducted? You had no contact with her after you kicked her out of her house, did you?"

"She told you I kicked her out?"

"She did."

"And you believed her, I suppose."

"Yes, I believed her. I believe her today. She's told me some of what you did to her, Racine, but there's a lot she won't talk about. A lot she *can't* talk about because it's just too traumatic for her."

"I'm sorry she feels that way, but don't you see?" She grabs my arm. "Everything will be okay now. She and I will have all the money in the world."

"And you don't think it's just a little bit odd that Kelly's father—if he is indeed her father—shows up now, while you happen to be in New York, tells you he's worth billions, and offers to give it to you?"

"He owes us, Leif."

I let out a laugh. "A lot of people owe me too, but I don't see them coming to me and offering me all their money."

"I don't know what else you want me to say."

"I want you to tell me what you're up to. Your daughter has been through enough. I won't allow—"

"Excuse me?" She scoffs. "You won't *allow*? I happen to be her mother—"

I look her dead in her eyes. "A mother wouldn't do what you did to her. I don't care if you gave birth to her. You don't deserve to be called her mother."

Racine's right eye twitches. "Kelly has always been imaginative. She likes to make up stories in her head."

"I don't doubt that that's true. She had a lot of time to think of them while she was locked in the closet."

Racine raises a hand. "I would never—"

I swat her hand aside. "Save it. We both know you're lying, Racine. What I didn't understand is why you've come back *now*. You're financially secure, you abandoned Kelly long ago, so why would you want to see her now? Then it became clear to me." I take a step toward her. "The father showed up. The father you wouldn't talk about when Kelly was little. The father you told me was never in the picture. Something doesn't add up here, Racine. The father *was* in the picture.

Maybe not during Kelly's childhood, but I'm betting he came to you sometime after she left home."

"He didn't."

"I say he did."

She looks at the floor. "You can say whatever you want, Mr. Ramsey, but you'll never prove anything like that."

"Maybe I won't. But I will do everything I can to protect Kelly. I'm in love with your daughter, and I will protect her. With my life if I have to."

Racine turns on her heel with a huff. "You tell Kelly she can find me at the Countess Regalia if she decides she wants the money from her father."

"The Countess Regalia?" I raise my eyebrows. "The Waldorf wasn't good enough for you?"

She doesn't reply.

"I'm not done talking to you," I say.

"Well I'm done listening." She pushes the button for the elevator.

It comes, and I get into it with her.

"Where did that two million come from five years ago, Racine?"

"What two million dollars?"

"Don't treat me like an idiot. You know damned well we had you checked out. Where did that money come from?"

She crosses her arms, taps her foot on the elevator floor. "I don't have to tell you anything."

"Then I'm going to venture a guess. Kelly's father— whoever he is—came to you then and gave you the money."

"You're full of it."

"Am I?"

"Yes, as a matter of fact you are. But so what if he did? It's no less than he owed me."

My guts twist into knots. I've seen the worst side of humanity, and now I'm understanding better why Kelly got so angry when I said there are no absolutes. I still believe that —and in a way, it helped me heal—but I also believe evil can cloud everything, take over everything.

Evil.

The evil of my own tormentors overseas.

The evil of Derek Wolfe and every man who went to that fucking island.

And the evil of the man who fathered Kelly.

It was him. And Racine, just as evil, took his money.

It's a theory, of course. Only a theory.

But it rings true.

It rings fucking true.

And I'd like to strangle the woman before me.

I grit my teeth.

"This isn't the first time you've had contact with him, is it? I'd be willing to bet you had contact with him over the years, starting before that first half a mill landed in your account."

She reddens. Tensing.

"You better tell me now. Because if you don't? I'm going to make your life fucking miserable. I will go to the authorities, and I will give them my theory about what *I* think happened to Kelly. Do you want me to do that?"

"Suit yourself."

The elevator doors open. But Racine makes no move to get out.

Interesting.

"After you," I say.

Still she doesn't move, and the doors close, the two of us still in the elevator.

"You have something you want to say to me?" I ask.

She tightens her lips. "I want your assurances of complete immunity."

"Immunity for what? You say you haven't done anything wrong."

"Damn it, Mr. Ramsey." She narrows her eyes. "It's clear that you care for my daughter. We have that in common."

"We *don't* have that in common, Racine. I know exactly how you treated your daughter."

"I've told you before how imaginative my daughter is. She was trapped on that island for five years, Mr. Ramsey. That messed her up. She probably created false memories."

I tamp down the rage. I won't get anywhere if I let it get the best of me. "Do you know that Kelly has a tattoo on her shoulder, Racine?"

"No."

"Tell me if this means anything to you. Kelly's tattoo is a picture of a volleyball surrounded by wilted black roses. Do you see any meaning there?"

Racine casts her gaze to the floor.

"I figured you would."

She looks up. "I was a single parent. I did the best I could."

"You keep telling yourself that. Tell it to yourself day in and day out. That won't make it true, but go ahead and do that."

"What do you want from me?"

"You stayed in the elevator," I say.

She twists her lips, says nothing.

"Tell me where the five hundred thou came from."

"It came after Kelly was taken."

"Yes, Racine, I know that."

"So if you're suggesting—"

"I'm not suggesting anything. But I'll be happy to tell you my theory if you want to hear it."

Racine taps one of her platform-heeled feet. "Please. I need immunity."

"Do I look like a district attorney to you? That's the only person who can grant you immunity. And quite frankly, if you did what I think you did?" I take one step closer to her. "You're never going to get immunity. Besides, you're forgetting one thing."

Her eyes widen slightly. "What's that?"

"You haven't been charged with anything yet."

"You're damned right I haven't." The door opens again, and Racine pushes out, her platforms tapping on the tiled floor of the lobby of the Wolfe building.

I pull out my phone, call Reid. "She's leaving the building now. Have her watched."

"I'm already on it." Reid says.

I end the call and return to the elevator. Time to go back to Kelly.

25

KELLY

About ten minutes later, Leif returns to the conference room.

I let out a breath when I see his handsome face. I didn't realize I'd been holding it until now. He's my solace. My strength. My safe place.

And damn, it irks me.

I've never depended on anyone. Not during my childhood, not after my mother kicked me out, and not on the island. I did what I had to do in order to survive, without help from anyone.

Some of the girls on the island were close to our house mother, Diamond. Not me. Diamond and I rarely interacted. We only spoke once, when I was in the infirmary after my thighs were cut.

Leif sits down and takes my hand. "Racine wants immunity."

Rock drops his jaw. "Say what?"

"I know, right?" Leif says. "She hasn't been charged with anything. She won't tell us anything. But obviously she's done something that she could go down for, so she wants immunity."

"Does she understand that none of us are in a position to grant her immunity?" Reid asks.

"Yeah. I made that clear."

"This is all such bullshit," I say.

"I know, sweetheart."

Reid and Rock both stare at Leif when he uses the word sweetheart.

He looks to the ceiling. "Okay, okay. I pulled a Buck Moreno. I fell in love with my charge."

"For Christ's sake." Rock rakes his fingers through his hair. "So that kiss on her cheek wasn't a fluke."

"It's unprofessional, I know," he says.

"What's done is done," Reid says. "I can't say much. I fell in love with one of my father's victims too."

Their eyes are all on me. I know what they're thinking. Sure, Reid fell in love with Zee, and Buck fell in love with Aspen. But Zee and Aspen are both nice people.

Me? I'm *not* a nice person. I've driven them all crazy. Made their lives hell.

Yet they let me be me. They feel responsible because I'm one of their father's victims, even though none of this is their fault.

Except for maybe the lapse in security the other night when The Dark One was able to breach the building. But they're working on that. Pretty soon the place will be like Fort Knox.

And I'm... I'm okay. Sure, I'm freaked out. Fucked up in the head, no doubt. But I'm unharmed. Physically at least.

"I tried to get information out of her," Leif says. "I asked her where the two million came from. I get the feeling she wants to talk. But she knows she's done something wrong, and she wants immunity before she talks."

"All she wants is this guy's money," I say.

"Oh, yeah, she definitely wants the money," Leif agrees. "But she may be banking on…"

"I see where you're going," Rock says. "Kelly, if you're truly this man's daughter, you're his next of kin."

"He could have other children," Lacey says.

Leif rubs his chin. "If what Racine said is true—and that's a big *if*—and he truly wants to give his money to Racine and Kelly, that would seem to indicate that he has no other children. No other heirs."

"Maybe he doesn't have long to live," Lacey says.

"That's possible," Leif says. "But Racine didn't seem to indicate that."

"Would you guys listen to me for once?" I shrug. "How many times do I have to say it? She didn't hear anything past the millions of dollars. That's all she wants. If this man has close to a billion, and he offered it to her, then I swear to God she didn't hear the rest of the conversation. She may have been present, but in her head, she was trying to decide where she'd spend his money first."

"None of us know her as well as you do," Leif says.

"That's right, you don't."

"Kelly," he continues. "Your mother made a comment. I want you to know that I don't believe it, but I have to ask. You suffered a lot of trauma on the island. All the girls did. Is it possible that the memories of your childhood were fabricated during therapy? Fabricated as a way to help you deal with the trauma from the island?"

Anger seeps through my flesh. I lived everything. I remember it all as if it happened yesterday. "For God's sake, Leif. On what planet does that make any sense? Don't you think Macy and I have talked about that? She ruled it out. My memories are *mine*, damn it. Don't even try to take them away from me."

"There's no record of social services ever being called on your mother," Reid says.

"Because she never left a mark. And I never told anyone. I knew better. What do you think would've happened to me if I told social services? My mother would've made it sound like it was all my fault. That I was an unappreciative little girl who was lashing out at her mother. And on the off chance that the authorities didn't believe her, I'd be sent away. And sure, some foster homes are great. But others? I might have been walking into something worse. At least with my mother, I knew what to expect."

Leif stares at me. I mean really stares.

"You can't seriously be thinking I made it all up," I say. "I know I lash out. But... My God, you seriously don't believe me?"

In that instant, I'm a little girl again. Huddled in the closet. Getting hungry. Shivering, not against cold but against fear.

My flesh chills and goosebumps erupt.

"Honey, no." Leif puts his arm around me. "I don't believe her. But I had to ask."

I yank his arm off me, my flesh warming. I'm no longer in the closet. I will never go back into that closet again.

"I can put you in touch with the friend from high school

who took me in after my mother kicked me out when I turned eighteen."

"We've already been in touch with that friend," Reid said. "Your story checks out, Kelly."

"See? I don't make things up. I'm not a liar."

"Baby, no one was thinking—"

I rise, shove my chair toward the table. "I'm so out of here." I race to the door, leave the conference room.

Leif is on my heels, of course.

"Kelly, I can't let you go alone."

"I was only here to talk to my mother. She's gone, so now I want to go home, Leif. I just want to go home."

"All right." He pulls out his phone. "I'll let Reid know. But Kelly, we need to figure out what's going on. If this guy truly is your father, maybe I can meet with him. Get his DNA somehow."

"All right. But I don't want to see him."

"I wouldn't ask you to, but this means..."

"Means what, Leif?"

"It means, unfortunately, that I'm going to have to speak to your mother again."

She sighs, closes her eyes, and then steps on the elevator ahead of me.

"I'm sorry, but we have to find out if this guy is really your father. And if he is, I'm going to make him talk to me. I'm going to find out what the fuck is going on here, and where your mother got that money."

Back in Leif's apartment, I sit quietly as he dials the number on the card Racine gave him from a burner phone.

"Forrester Smith?" he says.

He's not on speaker so I can't hear the rest.

"My name is Leif Ramsey. I'm a friend of Racine Taylor's."

Pause.

"Hell no, I'm not an attorney. I'm her muscle. She's ready to meet with you to finalize the transfer."

Pause.

"Yeah, everything. She told me everything. It's a go. But before we meet, Mr. Smith—

A shudder surges through me at the name. Mr. Smith. The Dark One.

"—I need your assurance that this is totally off every record. No cops. No wires. No nothing."

Pause.

"Chill, man. I told you that she told me everything. But you don't expect me to proceed without caution, do you?"

Pause.

"Good. So we understand each other. Racine and I will meet you at her hotel. I'll text you the room number."

Pause.

"Nine p.m. is perfect. See you then. And Mr. Smith?"

Pause.

"Come alone."

I have chills skittering up my arms as Leif ends the phone call and then pulls up a travel app on his device.

"What are you doing?"

"I'm reserving a room at your mother's hotel. I can't use her room because she's not going to know I'm there. At least not until I get there. I'm using the app so I can choose my own room. There we go. Now I just text this room to Mr. Smith, and we're on."

He texts, and within a few seconds his phone dings.

"He got the text, and he'll be there."

"What will I do?" Kelly says.

"You'll come with me."

"No. I don't want to see him."

"Don't be silly. I reserved two rooms on the same floor. I'll secure you in one. I'll check it out first. You'll have a burner phone with all my numbers and you can get in touch with me at any time."

"When do we leave?"

"Check-in time is four o'clock. We will be there then. I want you secure in your room before this man shows up."

26

LEIF

I haven't told the Wolfes that I'm meeting with this guy. This is for Kelly and me, not them. I haven't told Racine either. I told Kelly I may have to speak to her mother, and that's still true, but I want to see what I can find out about this guy first.

Kelly gapes at me as I strap pistols not only around my shoulder but also my ankle.

"Guns scare me," she says.

"I'll tell you what. When all this is over, and it's just you and me together, I'll teach you how to shoot. Then you won't have to be scared of guns."

"I'm still scared of someone holding one on me."

I caress her cheek. "I'm going to check your room out from top to bottom. You're going to be perfectly safe, and I will only be a few doors away."

She nods.

Kelly doesn't like to appear frightened. But these last two days—these run-ins with that dark one from her past—have her on edge. For someone who is used to taking care of herself—probably even on the island—she's got her nerves in a bunch. Which is why she's coming with me tonight.

She might be safer here in the apartment, with all the extra security that Reid Wolfe has put in place since the incident, but she'll *feel* safer closer to me. I don't want her feeling frightened. I don't want her going through any more than she has to.

"I wish I already knew how to handle a gun," she says. "Then I'd take one with me."

"I'd feel a lot better if you knew how to use one too, but I have something for you." I head back to my bedroom, open a black leather bag that I keep on the floor of my closet, and pull out a couple cans of pepper spray. I bring them back and hand them to Kelly. "One spray of this in the eyes, and you'll stop any attacker."

"Pepper spray? I have pepper spray, Leif. The Wolfes gave it to me on day one." She shakes her head, trembling. "My purse was sitting right next to me on the counter when The Dark One came into the bathroom last night. But I couldn't think, Leif. I couldn't move. I could've easily grabbed it, sprayed him with it. If I had... If I had, this would be over. He'd be in custody. What was I thinking?"

I pull her to me. "Kelly, please. You didn't expect him to show up in the women's bathroom at The Glass House. No one expected that. Maybe we should have. Maybe *I* should have. But I didn't. Don't blame yourself for this. The most important thing is that he didn't hurt you. And we *will* get him, Kelly. I swear to God we will get him."

"Then why are you wasting time on my mother and my alleged father?"

"Because I have a theory, Kelly. I have a theory about why and how you were taken."

"Can you share with me?"

"If you'd like me to. It's only a theory, and I may be completely wrong."

"You think my mother has something to do with this, don't you?"

"That was my original thought, yes. But a few things didn't make sense. First of all, her payments didn't start until six months after you were taken captive. Second of all, a payment of two million in total is way more than any of the others received. Katelyn's and Aspen's abductors, for example."

"So what are you thinking now?"

"I'm thinking...that whoever this man is, whether he's your father or not, he may have had something to do with it. I think that money your mother got after you were taken somehow came from him."

"Why would he want to do that? Why would my own father want to send me to that horrid place?"

"If I had that kind of answer, I'd be as psychopathic as he is. I can only tell you this. Derek Wolfe himself molested his only daughter for years."

She drops her jaw. "But I don't understand."

"I don't either. It's just a hunch, Kelly. But I want to find out where your mother got that money. She's not being completely honest with us, and she knows something. I can feel it in my bones."

"What if you're wrong?"

"If I'm wrong, I'm wrong. But we'll still have come closer to figuring things out. Your mother is involved in this somehow. Why else would she show up now? She doesn't need us. She doesn't need you. She's worth thirty million dollars."

Kelly nods, hunching her shoulders. "You're right. Racine Taylor doesn't care about me. She never did."

I kiss her forehead. "I know that's hard for you."

She shrugs. "I suppose it should be. Subconsciously, I'm sure I'm curling up into a fetal position crying right now. But honestly, Leif, I was glad to be rid of the woman. I've never had any desire to see her since she threw me out on my eighteenth birthday. At least she didn't give me a deflated volleyball that year. Or anything else for that matter. Only my freedom."

"By the time this is over, my love, I promise that you'll have everything your heart ever desired."

"Everything?"

"Everything I can get for you, anyway." I smile and cup her soft cheek. "Are you ready, baby?"

She straightens her shoulders. "Yes, Leif. I'm ready."

AFTER SECURING Kelly in the room I booked for her, I order some food from room service. We eat in silence, she barely choking down her spaghetti and meatballs. I'm the same way with my porterhouse steak. It's cooked to perfection of course, and the mashed potatoes and green beans with almonds are delicious, but I find it hard to swallow as well.

Kelly finally pushes her plate away from her after she's managed to choke down about half of her meal.

"Good. You ate well. Do you want any of your cake for dessert?"

She looks at the dense almond cake and frowns. "Maybe later."

"I understand. There are a few hours before I have to meet your father. Want to watch a movie?"

She shakes her head.

The king-sized bed in the room beckons. "I suppose we could…"

"Yes, Leif. Please."

Making love to Kelly is never a chore. It won't be our normal angry passion. It will be slow. Slow, because that's the mood we're both in right now. We're in limbo. We don't know what will happen next.

She undresses for me slowly, and I follow suit. Then she takes the lead, grabbing my hand and taking me to the bed.

"What would you like, baby?" I ask.

"Just lie with me. Let me touch you. You touch me."

"Of course." I lie down on the bed, pull her down next to me.

She snuggles into my arms, her soft head on my shoulder. I wrap my arms around her, and I glide my fingers down her side and then up over her soft shoulder.

Perhaps we'll just lie together, and although my cock is hard as a rock, I can handle that.

So I'm very surprised when her warm hand cups my balls.

I breathe in deeply. "Baby…" I caress her soft hair, kiss her forehead.

She plays with my balls, palms one and then the other and then she moves her head off my shoulder, giving me access to her lips.

We kiss. Just soft pecks, smacks of our lips, as she continues rubbing my balls.

Then...

She takes my cock, grasps it, and she adds her other hand.

"God," I groan. "Feels good."

She brings her hand to her mouth, swirls her fingers in her mouth to wet them, and then goes back to my cock. With one hand, she's cupping my balls, and with the other she's gliding up and down my cock.

I close my eyes, let the feelings overtake me. I want to do something for her, but this feels too good. So slow, so romantic.

And I wonder... Has she done this to any man before me?

Doesn't matter. So I let the thought go. I float away as if on a soft breeze.

I bring my other hand over to her shoulder to caress her, rub her back as she continues to play with me.

I groan. It comes out of my mouth like a slow growl.

She answers with a sweet sigh of her own. Then she kisses me. Smacks her lips against mine and then kisses my chest, my nipples, all the while still toying with my cock.

Slowly and slowly she works me, and I move my hips in tandem with her movements.

"Baby, I need you. Need to touch you. Kiss you."

"Please... Let me..."

She continues, and I continue getting more and more turned on. I want to come inside her tight little pussy, but if this is what she needs—what she wants in this moment—I will give it to her.

Her hands, her fists, her fingers, her glorious touch...

"Yeah, baby. Faster. Just like that..."

She tightens her grip, quickens her movements, and—

"God, yes..." I come. I come on her hands. Onto my own belly.

Then she moves on top of me, presses her lips to mine, tangles her tongue with mine.

We kiss.

We kiss for a long time.

27

KELLY

L eif left at eight thirty, and it's creeping up on nine now—when he's supposed to meet my supposed father.

He made me get dressed before he left. He didn't want me lying in here naked in case he had to come get me quickly. I'm sitting on the couch in my room next to the table where my half-eaten spaghetti still sits, now cold and congealed.

Leif said not to put the room service out because he doesn't want anyone to know that we're here.

That anyone is here.

The piece of almond cake still sits on the tray as well—both pieces actually. Leif didn't eat his either. It's a flourless cake—just dense almonds and vanilla.

I take my fork, break off a piece, bring it to my mouth. It's delicious and creamy, heady almost, the nuttiness of the almonds with a touch of vanilla.

It cries out for a dry sparkling wine, like Prosecco.

Then I wonder... How do I even know if wine would go with an almond torte?

Doesn't matter. Who cares?

We weren't allowed to have alcohol on the island. We weren't allowed to have any kind of sedation. The men didn't want us compliant. They wanted us to run, to fight.

That's what they were paying for.

Sometimes the women would pay Diamond for a pill or a toke of weed. I didn't. I don't normally touch the stuff. I had a glass of Chianti with Buck and Aspen the other night, but normally, I don't indulge. I never have. It wasn't available in my house when I was young. If it was, my mother kept it locked away. Once she kicked me out and I eventually graduated high school and got the job at the diner, I didn't have the time or the money to drink alcohol or to do anything stronger.

Right now, though?

Something to calm my nerves would be nice. Really nice.

I take another bite of the cake, let it slide over my tongue.

It actually tastes good. I couldn't really taste the spaghetti and meatballs, which I'm sure was delicious. This is the Countess Regalia. It's only one room, but it has a sitting area and a king-size bed. Between the two is a lot of space. I put the fork down after that. I don't want to eat any more. I rise and pace around the room, trying to exercise my nerves away. My pace turns into a jog, and I keep it up for ten minutes at least.

But then I stop.

It's after nine o'clock now. About fifteen minutes after.

Leif is in a room just a couple doors down.

Has the man who claims to be my father arrived yet?

I don't know.

"You know me, *don't you, Opal?" The Dark One says.*

"*Yes, of course. You're Mr. Smith. You've come here many times to see me.*"

"*But not always to see you, Opal.*"

Jealousy erupts in the pit of my stomach.

"*That's true," I say.*

I learned a long time ago to always answer when Mr. Smith speaks to me. Otherwise, he brings out his knife.

Each time he makes the same threat.

I have a knife and a penis, and one of them is going inside you tonight.

He hasn't put the knife inside me. Not yet. But each time could be the first time...

I'm clad in a sundress. It's what he prefers. This one is blue to match my eyes, he says. Sometimes it's orange, red, or brown to match my hair, he says.

I'm also wearing shoes. Running shoes.

The Dark One likes me to run, but he doesn't always allow me to wear shoes. What's different about this time? I may never know.

He leads me out to a Jeep, helps me inside. To an untrained eye on any other island, we would be a couple, perhaps heading to a masquerade, based on what he's wearing. He helps me into the backseat. A driver sits in front.

But this isn't any run-of-the-mill island in the South Pacific. And The Dark One and I are not a couple.

I'm driven to the hunting ground. A tropical hunting ground.

The driver drops me off, never speaking to me.

And I begin walking. I'll be running soon enough when The Dark One shows up. For now...I walk.

I walk through the dense pathways. Above me the palm trees shelter me from the harsh sun, and around me the bright tropical flowers dance.

And I think to myself what a beautiful place this could be...if it weren't hell on earth.

28

LEIF

I open the door to the regal suite that I booked. A few doors down, Kelly is safely secured in a deluxe room.

In front of me stands a large man. As tall as I am, and nearly as muscular. He's wearing all black, and his eyes are dark, but his hair is threaded with gray.

Is he armed?

I'll find out soon enough.

"Mr. Smith?"

He frowns. "Depends on who's asking."

"I'm Leif Ramsey. We spoke on the phone, as you know."

Smith enters, and I close the door.

"I don't understand what this fuss is about. I simply want to give my wealth to my daughter and her mother."

"I work for some very wealthy men myself," I say. "They've never heard of you."

"I tend to stay under the radar," he says.

"Interesting. Can I offer you something to drink?"

Smith looks around the room. "Bourbon if you've got it."

"Absolutely." I walk to the bar and pour him a bourbon.

"You'll join me, won't you?" he says.

"Thank you, but no."

"Come on. I insist."

He heads to the bar himself and pours another bourbon. I keep my eye on him, watching for any misdirection, but I see nothing.

He hands me the bourbon.

"Thank you." I take a sip.

Only I don't. I didn't see him do anything suspicious, but I don't trust this man as far as I can throw him. He may have laced my bourbon with something—which is part of the reason I didn't want to drink in the first place. I also want to keep my wits, so I won't be drinking.

He takes a sip of his.

And whether he drinks it? I don't fucking care. I already have what I need. His lip print on the glass, which contains his DNA.

I grab the glass and look at it. "I'm so sorry. This glass is cloudy. Let me get you a new one." I throw the bourbon in the sink, put the glass in the cupboard above it, and pour another bourbon.

Smith takes a step toward me and raises his eyebrows. "You don't believe me?"

"Believe you about what?"

"I'm not a moron. I know you want my DNA. Now you have it. You'll find out I'm not lying. Kelly *is* my daughter."

"I guess the lab will tell us that."

"You could've just asked me." He chuckles. "I'd be happy to give you my DNA. If you've got a Q-tip in the bathroom I can give you cheek swab."

If he thinks I'm going into the bathroom and leaving him

unattended in here, he can think again. "The glass will do. Thanks."

"Your call."

"What kind of business are you in, Mr. Smith?" I ask.

"Foreign currency exchange mostly. I hit a jackpot about twenty years ago. Reached the tipping point. Now I just sit around waiting for checks to clear, and my net worth increases every year on its own."

"Foreign currency, huh?"

"Oh, yeah. You can make a killing. I mean, look at me."

Yeah, look at him. If he's telling the truth, and I'm not convinced he is. His clothing is basic black trousers and a black long-sleeved T-shirt, black sneakers. Nothing to indicate how wealthy he claims to be.

"So tell me why now, after all these years, you've decided you want to give your money away to your long-lost daughter and your baby mama?"

"Because, Mr. Ramsey, it seems that I'm dying."

I keep my expression neutral. "I'm sorry to hear that."

He inhales slowly. "I suppose we all have to go sometime."

"May I ask what's wrong?"

He taps the side of his head. "An inoperable brain tumor. It's not cancer. Totally benign, but it's fast-growing and within the next couple of months, dementia will set in, and soon my brain will be too damaged to function at all, and I'll be gone."

Again, I keep my expression noncommittal. I'm not at all convinced he's telling the truth. But I can easily find out if he is who he says he is. If that's the case, the Wolfes can hire someone to hack into his medical records, but I'm guessing Forrester Smith is an alias.

I'm still not convinced he's related to Kelly, either, but the DNA will crack that part of the story soon enough.

"There's nothing the doctors can do?"

"They've done all they can. They slowed the process enough to give me enough time to get my affairs in order."

"I see."

Smith walks toward the window and stares out of it. "You know, when you have to face your own mortality, you begin to see things in a different way."

"I know that."

"Pardon me, Mr. Ramsey, but you're young and healthy. I'm afraid you *don't* know that."

"You're wrong. I served my country as a Navy SEAL on several tours of duty, and I faced my mortality more than once. Believe me."

"Indeed?" He lifts his eyebrows. "Thank you for your service."

I resist the urge to drop my jaw at his comment. "You're welcome. It was an honor to serve my country."

Smith clears his throat. "I'm not looking for anyone's empathy. I haven't lived the best life, and I probably deserve what I'm getting."

"You mean for abandoning Kelly."

He moves from the window, stares around the large suite. "I didn't abandon her. I didn't know she existed. Not until about five or six years ago."

I lift my eyebrows. "I see. You might be interested to know that your—hell, I don't know what you call her, your baby mama?—says you only just got in contact with her recently."

"She's not telling the truth."

I can't help an eye roll. "There's a shocker."

"I owe her a lot," he says. "Taking care of our daughter when I wasn't there to do so."

"You don't owe her crap. From what I understand, she was a terrible mother."

"You don't say."

"And you don't seem too upset to hear that."

"Understand this from my position," he says. "Racine is a woman I had indiscriminate sex with at a masquerade party nearly thirty years ago. I had no feelings for the woman then, and I have no feelings for her now. As for my daughter, I don't know her. I want to get to know her. I'd like her to be a part of my life."

"Don't you think that's up to her?"

"Of course it is. But I don't have a lot of time left, Mr. Ramsey. Please, try to see it my way."

"I do see it your way," I say. "But that doesn't change things from Kelly's perspective."

He sighs. "I know."

The man is a pretty good actor. I'll give him that. He knows what to say and how to say it. But his body language speaks differently. There's something else at work here, and I'm going to figure out what it is.

Is he truly dying of an inoperable brain tumor? Or is that just a little too convenient?

"Tell me why you gave Racine two million dollars five years ago."

He meets my gaze. "Where did you get that idea?"

His expression shows some surprise—a raised brow, parted lips. But something is still off, and I can't quite put my finger on it.

"You're aware that Kelly was kidnapped and held on

Derek Wolfe's island, aren't you?"

He inhales. "I am. Very unfortunate."

His tone doesn't indicate any remorse, and although he doesn't know Kelly at all, he should still be disgusted by a young woman being taken to that place. What is his angle?

"Racine came into some money five years ago. About six months after Kelly was taken. It's a lot of money, Mr. Smith. Two million paid over the course of a year. She won't divulge how she got it, but I have the best investigators on it, and we *will* find out."

"I wouldn't know anything about that. I do know that Racine's not hurting for money right now."

"That's right. She's not. Thanks to that two mill and some estate from a childless aunt. So why does she want *your* money?"

Smith's lips curve slightly upward. "With all due respect, I have a lot more money than she does."

"Why didn't you use your money to try to find your daughter when she disappeared?"

"Who says I didn't?"

He could be telling the truth. Others exhausted their resources looking for those women. Derek Wolfe made sure they were untraceable. Still, I'm not buying.

I'm tempted to draw my gun, but if the man is truly facing dementia, he may be just as happy to go quickly.

I need to check on Kelly anyway.

"Could you excuse me for a moment?"

"Of course—" He rises, but then he loses his footing.

I grab his arm for support. "Are you all right?"

His hands tremble. "Yes, yes. I'm fine. Could you just get me some water, please?"

"Of course."

29

KELLY

He catches me, as he always does.

And then he hovers on top of me, scooting my dress up my thighs until I'm exposed to him.

The mask covers his face, but his dark eyes bore into me.

The cool steel of the knife against my neck is oddly pleasurable. After being chased in a tropical climate, anything cool feels good.

He scrapes it against my skin.

I have a knife and a penis, and one of them is going inside you tonight.

I close my eyes.

"Open your eyes," he demands.

I open them, and—

I JERK UPWARD, still on the couch. The subtle sound of the lock on the door being engaged.

My heart is pumping wildly. "Leif?"

Thank God he's back.

The door opens, and I rise—

"No!"

A masked man dressed all in black charges me, and I—

We're on a high floor.

I have nowhere to go.

But I run anyway. I run as if I'm on the island, being hunted.

I run toward the window—

Strong arms grab me from behind, and then a poke to my neck—

And everything fades to black.

30

LEIF

Whoever the hell this man is, he's taking forever to drink this water.

He takes a sip, and then he closes his eyes, breathes in and breathes out.

Then he opens his eyes, another sip.

I need to get to Kelly. Check on her.

I grab my phone, text her quickly.

Just checking in.

I expect her to text right back, and when I don't get one, worry pulses through me.

"If you'll excuse me," I say, "I need to leave for a moment."

"Yes, I'm fine. I just need to sit here a bit."

"Sure, of course." I walk to the cupboard by the bar, grab the glass with his DNA on it because yeah, I don't trust the guy, and then leave and walk a few doors down to the room where Kelly is.

"Kelly, it's me," I say as I knock softly. "I'm coming in now."

I let the key card hover over the lock, and the green light clicks on. I walk in.

"Kelly? Baby?"

Perhaps she went to bed.

But she's not in the bed.

She's not in the bathroom either.

No sign of a struggle.

This is Kelly. Kelly, who doesn't always follow orders. Who probably just went down the hallway to get some ice.

Kelly, who—

Except my blood is running cold, like ice water in my veins. My pulse is racing, and I know...

I know she didn't leave this room of her own volition.

Kelly, where are you?

An image surges into my mind. An image of that poor girl, Brindley, on the bed, blood oozing from her, her skin already turning yellowish in death

Only it's not Brindley lying there.

It's my Kelly.

I've learned never to ignore my hunches. I don't know if this man claiming to be her father is the person who killed Brindley, but I know he's involved in some way.

I just need to figure out how.

"Oh, Kelly," I choke back a tear. "I was supposed to protect you. How could I have failed you?"

I got cocky. That's what it was.

I'm Phoenix. Phoenix always rises from the ashes.

Except I'm not a mythical bird, and I'd do well to remember that.

Now I know how Buck felt when he couldn't protect Amira in Afghanistan. How Ace felt when he lost his woman.

My God, a knife has sliced my heart in two.

But I don't have time to dwell on it. I get on the phone, call 911 and report the situation. Then I call Reid.

"You left her alone?" Reid says.

"In a hotel room. Secure. And somehow—"

"We didn't give you any authority to meet with this guy."

"I don't take orders from you. Kelly is my responsibility, and I wanted to find out what was going on."

"I understand that. I understand how you feel about her, believe me I do. The same way I feel about Zee. But Leif—"

"I'm not in the mood for a dressing down right now, Reid. I need to fucking find her."

"We'll find her. We're already on it."

"What the hell is that supposed to mean?"

"It means I know where you went."

"And you knew I took her with me."

"That's right."

"So it's not enough to have me watching her. You're watching me as well."

"Only since the apartment building security was compromised. Only since Brindley was killed."

I open my mouth to argue...but why? The main thing is that they're already working on finding Kelly.

"Whoever is behind this is some kind of Houdini," Reid says. "How he's able to get past our security is beyond me. And that can only mean..."

I sigh. "Someone on the inside."

"Yes," Reid says. "And now I have to find out who it is."

"Just find Kelly. Please. She can't end up like Brindley. She just can't."

"She won't. I swear to God I'll die first."

"Not before I do," I say. "I swore I'd protect her, and I can't let her down."

"I'll be in touch." Reid ends the call.

Damn right he'll be in touch.

In the meantime, what do *I* do? I can't just sit here. I rush back to the other room. Time to interrogate this Mr. Smith.

Except, when I get there?

He's fucking gone.

I want to bang my head against the wall. Scream in rage. Let the tears inside me fall.

But I can't.

Now is not the time for emotional outbursts.

Now is the time for action.

And I know what to do when it's time for action.

If only Buck were in town, the two of us could work together. But he's not, so this is a solo mission.

And I will not fail.

I *cannot* fail.

I can't fail Kelly.

I will find her. And I will fucking find her tonight.

I head back to the hotel room, and I thoroughly search for clues.

Damn.

Nothing.

Whoever is doing this is more than a professional. He's an escape artist.

How did he get Kelly out of here? We're on a high floor. I look at the balcony. Open the sliding glass doors.

Look down.

It's dark outside, but I look closely. Nothing. If he had escaped this way, someone would have seen him. Plus, how the hell could he get down on a rope or whatever else carrying a woman? She would be screaming and thrashing and—

No. She'd be drugged.

Fucking bastard drugged my Kelly.

And Mr. Smith? I don't know whether he's Kelly's father or not, but he's no friend to her.

I walk briskly back through the place, ready to devise a plan, when several uniformed police officers walk through the open door.

Shit. I'm the one who called them, but I don't have time for this now.

"What happened, sir?"

"My...girlfriend. She was in this room. Now she's gone."

"And you don't think she left of her own accord?"

"I know she didn't. Kelly Taylor. Check with your fellow officers. She's been questioned with regard to security breaches at the Wolfe residential building in the area. I don't have time to answer questions right now. I need to go find her."

"You realize we can't file a missing persons report until twenty-four hours have passed."

"Fine. Fine. Just comb this place for fingerprints or whatever you do. I need to go." I brush past them, pushing them out of the way.

"Sir, stop right now."

I turn. One of them has a gun pointed at me.

You've got to be kidding me.

I raise my hands. "Look, I don't want any trouble. But I love this woman, and I'm going to find her. I'm her best chance right now, and if you shoot me, I won't be able to do what I need to do."

"Sir, you will not leave until you answer some questions."

I don't take police for granted, but right now, Kelly is more important than following their orders. I serpentine down the hall to the stairwell, hoping he won't try to hit a moving target.

He doesn't, thank God.

I could've pulled out one of my own pieces, but that would've just taken more time.

I scurry down the stairwell, floor after floor, until I finally hit the first floor, rush through the lobby, and outside.

Now what?

I don't know where to look.

I don't even know what to—

Until I drop my gaze to the sidewalk.

It's a phone.

A burner phone.

I pick it up, and a text message is flashing.

Damn. For a moment I thought this might be Kelly's burner phone that I gave her. But it's not. Someone else's.

I throw it back on the ground and look up, raking my fingers through my hair, thinking, thinking, thinking...

And I see it.

The camera perched near the side of the hotel.

Is it a traffic camera? Or is it part of the hotel security?

It blends in with the decor so well that if I didn't know what I was looking for, I may not have seen it.

Whoever has been tormenting Kelly is either a magician —or has someone working on the inside.

Since no one is a magician of that caliber, he's got

someone on the inside for sure. Which means...he probably didn't notice that camera.

I race back inside the hotel. No one's at the concierge desk, so I run to the check-in counter, bumping people in line.

"Hey, what the fuck do you think you're doing?" a belligerent man yells.

"Shut up. I've got a missing woman on my hands."

He steps back obediently. "Sorry."

"That camera outside. I need the footage from it. Now."

The check-in clerk, a young woman with pale blond hair, widens her eyes. "Sir, what camera? I don't know what you're—"

"I don't have time for this. Give me the manager."

She nods quickly, running into the back.

An older woman with silver streaking her light brown hair returns. "I'm Lenore. I'm the manager on duty this evening."

"That camera outside over the door of the hotel. I need the footage."

"May I ask what for?"

"Didn't you see the police come in? Did they talk to you? A woman has been kidnapped from one of your rooms."

Lenore steps back. "What? My God!"

"Yes, I work for the Wolfe family. I need that footage."

"Let me find our security team."

"What do you mean, find your security team? Don't you know where they are?"

The woman is obviously flustered. "Yes, of course. Let me do what I can." She pulls her cell phone from her pocket.

I call Reid. "Reid? It's me, Leif. I need you to talk to this hotel manager. There's a camera outside that may have seen where they took Kelly."

"Unless they went out a back door."

"Right." I turn to Lenore. "Do you have cameras on all your points of egress?"

"We do."

"I need all that footage. Here, talk to Mr. Wolfe." I hand the phone to Lenore.

Reid is dominating their conversation, because all Lenore says is "yes, sir" several times. Until she hands me back the phone.

"Did you get it?"

"Yeah. She's going to have her security team pull up all the footage for the last couple hours."

"Great. God, I hope we see something."

"I do too."

"By the way, you need to call the cops off. They stopped me, held a fucking gun on me up in the room I booked for Kelly. Wanted me to stay to answer some questions, but I don't have time for that."

"I'll see that it's taken care of."

"Thanks."

I hate standing around. My pulse is racing, and my whole body is in fight-or-flight. I need to protect Kelly. Need to find her. Need to save her.

But my best chance at knowing where to go is this security footage.

So I have no choice.

I wait.

31

KELLY

oving.

I think I'm moving.

But I seem to be floating as well.

Can't feel my body.

Not sure where I am... Where... I... Am...

Aren't you going to say thank you, Kelly?

Aren't you going to say thank you for the thoughtful gift I gave you?

It's your eighteenth birthday today. Don't bother coming home from school. Get out.

Didn't I tell you not to be here when I got home? You're eighteen now! Get out, or I'll call the cops on you for trespassing!

You're twelve today. Have you started your menstruation yet?

You're not a grown-up. Fifteen today, and you're still not menstruating.

I wake up, my stomach cramping.

Blood stains my white sheets.

Three days after my fifteenth birthday. Such a late bloomer.

My mom will be angry with the blood on my sheets. So I get up quickly, strip my bed, until—

Kelly. What are you doing?

I'm...changing my sheets, mama.

Whatever for? Didn't you just change them three days ago when I told you to?

She brushes past me, grabs the sheets, looks at them.

The blood.

So you're a woman after all, Kelly.

She raises her hand... Wants to hit me...

But I'm as big as she is now.

Still, she's my mother...

You should always obey your mother...

Even when she's a vicious bitch like mine is.

But I walk past her.

I walk past her with no place to go. If only I had some money. Or enough to eat to give myself the strength I need.

I can never play volleyball.

Never bothered trying out for the team.

I gave it up, after she destroyed my volleyball when I was ten.

And at this point?

I'll never have the strength...

Never have the strength...

Never have the strength...

I'm running... Running... Running...

He'll catch me. He always does.

But still I run. We have to run. It's what they want.

And here on the island, they always get what they want.

32

LEIF

I pound my fist into the wall. "What the fuck do you mean the tapes are blank?"

The security man's name is Jake. He looks about nineteen. "I'm sorry, sir. We must've had a glitch."

"The only glitch is in your fucking head." I grab his shoulders and yank him out of his chair. "How much are they paying you? What are they paying you to fuck up the tapes?"

"Sir, I don't know what you're—"

My fist hits his chin with a thud. I went easy on him, and still he's on the floor.

I sit down at his desk.

"Sir, I can't let you—"

"Shut the fuck up."

It's been a while, but I know my way around security software. I tap on the computer, move some things around and—

There it is.

Security footage from all cameras for the last couple hours.

"You son of a bitch," I say.

Jake rises slowly into a sitting position, rubbing his chin. "I had to. I was supposed to erase them, but you..." He rubs his forehead, tears glistening in his eyes. "He threatened my family."

"Yeah? Well he's *got* my family. Who is it? Who threatened you?"

"I don't know. It all came by phone. He said—"

"I don't give a fuck what he said. You can tell it to the cops. Right now I need to find the relevant footage." Thank God I got to him before he erased the footage. I scan through the alternate doors first, thinking he wouldn't go out the front door.

Nothing.

How the hell did he get out of here? With Kelly?

I pull up the footage for the main door.

Nothing.

Nothing unusual at all. No Kelly. And no suitcase or satchel big enough for her to be in.

Which means...

The threat to the security tech was a ruse. With no footage, we'd assume they left the building, and all the while...

I turn back to the manager. "They're still here," I say through gritted teeth. "You're going to need to lock down this place."

"We're at seventy-five percent capacity right now, sir," she says. "I can't."

"Most of them are probably already in their beds," I say. "Lock it down."

"I can't do that on your authority." She narrows her eyes. "Who are you anyway?"

In a flash, my gun is out of my ankle holster and trained on her. "I'm the person with a gun to your head. Now do as I say and lock this fucking place down."

She gulps. The security computer tech is still on the floor rubbing his jaw. When he sees the gun, he yells.

"Just lock it down. Someone has my girlfriend. Someone's been after her. Whoever it is already killed another. A young girl. Murdered her in cold blood, and he's after my girlfriend, Kelly Taylor. Please. For the love of God. I don't like doing this, but you've got to lock this place down."

She nods, trembling. Then she pulls out her phone and taps on it. "Nesbitt, it's Lenore. We've got a missing woman. We need to lock down."

Pause.

"What do you mean on whose orders? On *my* orders."

Pause.

"Yeah, the police are here. They're up on ten, investigating the same situation."

Pause.

"No footage of anybody leaving, so we're locking down. We're going to have to check all the rooms."

Pause.

"Right. I'm on it." She ends the call. Then to me, "Nesbitt, my head of security, says to call in the SWAT team." She motions to another employee.

I'll find you, Kelly.

I promised I would protect you, and I will.

33

KELLY

hat's it, precious. Time to wake up now.

Words.

Words make it into my head.

Come on. You can do it.

My neck hurts. Something poked me. That's nothing compared to the pounding inside my head. As if two hatchets have sliced my head open, right between the ears.

I see things. Are my eyes open?

I flutter my eyelids. Images. Blurred images.

A person. Two people.

There you go, baby. Wake up like a good girl.

Baby? Only Leif has ever called me baby, but this is not his voice. Leif... He was coming to check on me... I heard him open the door, and then—

I don't remember anything after that.

Where am I?

My heart... I think it wants to beat... I think it wants to beat like crazy...

But my body is limp. Can't seem to move.

That should scare me, but I don't feel scared.

Drugs.

Must be drugs.

Is this what drugs feel like? I wouldn't know. I've never used them. The only other time...

After throwing up the tainted chocolate at work, and I woke up in a concrete room. Drugs. It felt different that time, but it had to be drugs.

She's awake.

Are you sure?

Her eyes are open. Sort of.

Does she act like she hears you?

No, but it'll take a little while for the shot to wear off.

All right. Ramsey will know by now that she's gone. We need to lie low until it's safe.

Ramsey?

Leif?

Leif doesn't know I'm here?

I open my mouth to yell, but my lips don't move. My voice doesn't work.

I flutter my eyes again. Try to get a better look at the men who have me.

I should be scared. Angry and scared. And I am...

But I can't feel it.

I can't fucking feel it.

What should we do with her now?

We can't leave her until she's fully conscious.

You think she's going to go willingly?

She will. She's not going to have a choice.

No, I have a choice.

But I can't say it. Can't move.

Oh my God, I can't even feel.

Numb, so numb. All those years when I prayed for numbness.

Now it's here... Now I know what it's like to feel, and I don't want to be numb anymore.

I want to feel... I want the love and sweetness and everything else that Leif has taught me.

And I want the anger. The anger and the vengeance. I want to feel the rage for these people who have taken me against my will.

They took me.

Leif, where are you?

I will get back to him.

Or he will find me.

He'll never give up until he finds me.

But I have to help him. I can't just react like I normally do. I have to be proactive, but how can I be, when I can't get my voice to work? My body to work?

Someone touches me then.

I want to slink away, but I can't. My body doesn't work.

What the hell have they done to me? Where's Leif? My Leif?

Come on, precious. It's time.

I flutter my eyes again.

She is awake.

Then why isn't she moving?

Someone pushes against my body.

And I feel it yet I don't.

Help! Help! Help!

How I want to scream, run, find Leif.

But nothing works. It's like I'm trapped in a block of ice or something. I feel it when he touches me, but I can't move.

Leif... Leif... Leif...

We have to get ready to go. They're starting to search the place. We were supposed to be out of here before that happened.

Yeah, well, the dude on security must've screwed us over.

Yeah? Then he'll pay.

He was supposed to destroy the damned tapes.

That's what he said he'd do, but he must've forgot to disable the backup. These days all systems have a backup to the backup.

Damn it.

How the hell do we get out of here? Especially if she doesn't wake the fuck up?

We'll need to hide in plain sight.

How exactly can we do that with an unconscious woman? And she's not going to be cooperative when she comes to.

She'll be cooperative. She and I are old friends.

Old friends?

Hear that, Kelly? You and I are old friends. I have a knife and a penis, and onc of them is going inside you tonight.

The voice.

It's not The Dark One.

Or is it?

My head is so fuzzy. I don't know what's up and what's down. All I know is that I should be scared and I am. But I don't feel it. Something is keeping me from feeling. This numbness. It's like being in an ocean with no waves.

I flutter my eyelids one more time. Trying to wake up. Trying to feel. Something. Right now I want all the negative feelings. I want my anger and my rage and my terror.

I'll take her.

We could go on the service elevator.

They're probably locked down by now.

Lockdown?

Leif? Where are you, Leif?

Leif won't leave any stone unturned. Wherever we are, he will find me. I have to believe that.

Because my story doesn't end this way. It doesn't end with numbness. It doesn't end with me not fighting back.

My story ends with Leif. Leif and me together.

Now that I finally have something to live for, I want to live. I want to feel.

My eyes pop open then.

Three figures.

So you're awake, precious.

Only two figures. Then three again. My eyes are blurred, fatigued.

She's coming to, Ronald.

Another figure approaches me.

This one I know.

The Dark One.

"There you are, Kelly. You need to get up now. We have places to go."

Now I recognize the voice.

"I'm not going anywhere with you."

Except the words don't come out. They sound like a croaking frog.

"Don't try to talk yet, precious. There's someone here who wants to meet you."

The other person comes close. "Hello, Kelly. My name is Forrester Smith, and I'm your father."

34

LEIF

Reid has arrived, and he along with the SWAT team are the only people who've been allowed into the hotel since the lockdown.

He and I are sitting in the lobby, along with the manager of the hotel and Jake, the young security guard who tried to finagle the tapes. He's being questioned by one of the officers.

"It was all via phone." Jake hands them his phone. "You can see it here. Maybe you can trace a number."

"It's most likely untraceable," an officer says.

"You can see. He knew things about my children that no one could know. He... I had no choice, Officer. You've got to believe me."

"I do believe you, sir," the officer says.

I get it. I do. If someone threatened Kelly or one of my sisters, I'd do anything to protect them. But right now I have a hard time feeling sorry for the guy.

At least we know now that they didn't leave the building. If he had succeeded in destroying the backup recordings for the time in question, we'd be out on a wild goose chase when she's actually still here in the hotel.

The police officer continues to ask him questions, and he answers, still trembling.

"I made arrangements for Brindley's remains today," Reid says. "That was difficult."

I suppose I should feel for him. On a normal day I would. That beautiful young girl certainly didn't deserve to come to such a grisly end. No one ever loved her.

Right now? The only thing on my mind is Kelly.

She's here.

And now that I know for sure that she is? I feel her. I feel her presence.

I didn't before.

I don't dare mention this to Reid. He'll think I'm nuts. But I feel her now. She's alive. I will get to her.

My phone buzzes.

Buck.

"Hey," I say into the phone.

"Hey, I just heard from Reid. You doing okay?"

"Fuck, no. But I can handle it."

"You want me to head back?"

"No, man. Stay with Aspen and her family. Take care of business. This is my problem, not yours."

"Hey, your problems are my problems. Brothers forever." His voice breaks slightly. "Buck and Phoenix, the only ones left."

"Right... Take care of your woman, man. And I'll try like hell to take care of mine."

"I'm sorry, Phoenix. I didn't realize how hard you'd fallen."

"I didn't either. But I have. I love her, man. I swore to protect her, and I..." I can't go on.

"Phoenix always rises," he says.

"Yeah, the Phoenix does. But she's not the Phoenix, Buck. She's Kelly. The woman I love."

"Don't do this to yourself. You took care of her as well as anyone could have."

"Whoever this dude is, he's got money. Money enough to pay off security people. Money enough to get information to blackmail people."

"I doubt he has as much money as the Wolfes."

"What the fuck does that matter? He's done what he's done, and now Kelly's gone. I need to get to her. She's somewhere in this damned hotel."

"Then you'll find her."

"I sure hope so." A chill slithers up my spine. "I mean, I know I'll find her. I just hope I find her before it's too late."

"You will."

"This person, the stalker... He fucking killed Brindley, Buck. He shoved a knife into her cunt and killed her."

Buck stays quiet.

What the hell can he say?

"That won't happen to Kelly," he says. "From what the Wolfes told me, he has some kind of attachment to her. Brindley was just a message."

"Brindley wasn't a message, Buck. Brindley was a young woman. A young woman who had a shitty life, and that's all she'll remember."

Again, no response from Buck. Until—

"I'm coming out."

"No. You take care of your wife. That's what's important.

Believe me, now I know better than ever how important that is."

"You sure?"

"I'm sure. Thanks for the offer, man."

We end the call, and I watch as the black-clad SWAT team moves in. They will find her. Right now, whoever has her doesn't realize that we know she's in the hotel, so they won't be watching their backs.

Reid is busy talking to police officers and the manager. The few employees who are still around are trembling, looking back and forth.

No one's paying any attention to me, so I use that to my advantage.

I head toward the stairwell and slip inside.

35

KELLY

The eyes.

As my vision clears, his eyes come into focus.

Dark eyes...but different. Not the eyes that tormented me on the island and continue to torment me now.

Still... Dark...

"Can you understand me, Kelly? I said I'm your father."

The eyes...

His voice seems familiar...

But then the voice...

"Remember me, Kelly?"

I have a knife...

That's the voice.

He's in this room... In this room with the man who claims to be my father.

"Who is that?" I eke out.

I'm not sure if the words make any sense, as my voice is still shot and not quite my own.

The eyes...

Always the eyes...

Even on the island I felt like his eyes were familiar.

Images flash backward in my mind, as if a film is rewinding.

And I'm there.

There on that last day in the restaurant.

When I took over Georgianna's shift. Was that all preconceived?

Because the man from her section, who left the chocolate... Oh my God.

That man...

That man was my father.

"You can't be my father," I say.

"I assure you I can, and I am."

"Then why are you hanging around with someone who likes to hurt me? And why did you... Why did you..."

"Why did I what?"

"You poisoned me with that chocolate. All those years ago. You left the chocolate with your tip."

"Everything will make sense to you in time, Kelly," my father—if he is indeed my father—says.

"Who was that other guy? Who is The Dark One? Why does he call himself Mr. Smith?"

"Because his name *is* Mr. Smith, Kelly. He's my son."

Nausea creeps up my throat. I retch, but nothing comes up.

"If... If... If..."

"I think what you're trying to say," Smith says, "is that if he's my son, that also makes him your brother."

I retch again, my stomach cramping, my flesh erupting in goosebumps.

Brother? I have a brother? And father? And my brother...
It's too sick to even contemplate.

"What's the story?" I manage to get out before I retch again.

"No story, Kelly," the one who claims to be my father says. "I didn't know you existed until you had already left your mother's house. Your brother and I came to the diner every so often, and well, your brother..."

"You're mine," The Dark One says. "Mine not only by blood."

"Aren't fathers supposed to protect their daughters? And aren't brothers supposed to protect their sisters?"

"Obsession runs deep," my father says. "I couldn't stop your brother, so I gave you to him. I let him take you to that island. I had to pay off your mother for her silence, but she was more than willing to take my money. I let him have you. Because I knew, if you ever got off that island, you'd have a better life than working long hours at a diner."

"Yeah. That's what you are all right. Altruistic." I choke back nausea. "Leif will find me."

"Leif is scouring the city for you," The Dark One says.

"They're already on lockdown, Ronald," the other one says. "They—"

"Leif has no idea that you're still here in the hotel," the Dark One continues, speaking over his supposed father. "He doesn't care about you, Kelly. He never cared about you."

Only...he swore to protect me...

Has he forsaken me? Does he not love me anymore?

No.

The word comes to me so quickly I don't even realize it.

No, Leif has not forsaken me. And yes, Leif still loves me.

He saw something lovable in me, and that must mean it's there. Because Leif—strong, dependable, good Leif—wouldn't be able to love someone who's unlovable.

"He'll come. He'll figure it out."

"By the time he figures it out, we will be long gone," The Dark One says. "Now, Kelly, *I have a knife and a penis, and one of them is going inside you tonight.*"

I brace myself, ready to kick the shit out of The Dark One, until my father pulls him back.

"No. I've allowed you to have her, Ronald, but I will not watch it."

While I hate my father with a purple passion—he and his son are completely psychotic and demented—I'm grateful to be spared in this moment.

God... What kind of sick genetics do I come from?

My mother...and this? An absent father who gives me away to a psycho half-brother?

And a psycho half-brother who's obsessed with me? Who gets off on sending his sister to hell on earth and then violating her repeatedly? I can only hope the worst of him comes from his mother's side.

Leif, please hurry.

Please...

36

LEIF

I'm surprised the stairwells are open. The SWAT team should have locked them. Or…instructed the manager to do it.

I return to Lenore.

"The stairwells aren't locked down," I say.

"They should be," she says. "I gave instructions to—"

"Whoever you gave instructions to isn't listening to you. Whoever has my woman up there has someone on the inside. We already know they tried to blackmail the tech guy who was manning the cameras. There's someone else—it could be someone standing right here—helping these people."

"I don't have to stand here and take this kind of insult," the manager says.

"You don't have to take anything," Reid says to her, "but I can tell you that my family does a lot of business with this hotel. I trust Leif. If he says there's someone on the inside working with these guys, I want you to take it seriously."

"I have full trust and faith in my staff," she says.

"I'm sure you do. The best spies are those you would never suspect." I grip my hands together. "For example, who's in charge of locking down in the case of an emergency?"

"My security chief, of course. Lyle Nesbitt."

"And where is he?"

"He's fully armed, so he's most likely with the SWAT team."

"I don't think so," I say. "I don't care how handy the guy is. No SWAT team wants a civilian hanging around."

The manager simply bites her lip.

"Where's Nesbitt, anyway?"

"He was here a little while ago. He talked to the cops."

"He's not here now." I look around. "Just the officers, Mr. Wolfe here, and you."

"We *are* in a lockdown. I've instructed most of the employees to go to the conference center on this floor. It's big enough to hold all the employees, and they'll be safe there, locked in, until this is taken care of."

"I see. So where is that chief of security, then? Surely he didn't run like a scared rabbit to the conference center with the rest of the employees."

"He's the night security chief," she says. "It is the middle of the night, or haven't you noticed?"

"I don't know whether it's night or day anymore, for the amount of sleep I've gotten." I say.

"It's the night guy, Nesbitt. I know him well. He's a decent human being. I trust him implicitly."

"Do you trust all the guys who work under him?" I ask. "Someone isn't doing their job, or the stairwells would've been locked off."

Lenore says nothing. What can she say? I'm a hundred percent right.

One of the officers regards the manager. "We're going to need to talk to this Nesbitt again."

"You're welcome to, but I don't know where the hell he is." She taps on her phone. "I'm getting those stairwells locked now."

"Doesn't seem like things are going by the book here," Reid says.

"I don't know what your security guidelines are here, ma'am," one of the officers says. "I don't think it's going very well."

"Shit." I rub my hand over my forehead. "If someone from hotel security is indeed working with the guys upstairs, then he's already alerted them to the fact that we know they're still here."

"Leif," Reid says, "don't go off halfcocked."

"What the hell would you have me do? A bunch of derelicts are up there holding my woman captive. These aren't nice men, Reid. You know what kind of men they are. The kind of men who visited your father's infamous island."

Reid's cheeks redden. He's angry, but I don't care. I don't blame him for what his father did. I never have. But right now? Right now they have Kelly. People who probably were on that island, violating her in unthinkable ways.

And I'm tired of it. I am tired of being in danger, but more than that? I'm tired of my woman being in danger.

We've already lost one.

What happened to Brindley will *not* happen to Kelly.

But I'm helpless. Helpless. I can't go after the SWAT team,

and I can't even go up to the floors and search myself because the building's on lockdown. The elevators are locked. The stairwells should be locked by now. All the doors are fucking locked.

I'm fucking helpless.

Just like that day...

That day when I heard Wolf die.

But I didn't stay helpless for long.

*T*HIS ONE WEARS SUNGLASSES.

He wears sunglasses inside, and I don't know why. I don't care why.

But those sunglasses give me an idea.

The place smells. Smells of stale urine and my own shit. But I eat the crust of bread the fuckers brought to me. I eat it while the guard watches me. Taunts me in broken English.

"You think you tough, SEAL. You think you so tough."

Wolf is gone, but so help me, I won't let the same thing happen to Buck. My hands are cuffed together, but at least I'm not hanging.

So I look down. I don't meet the fucker's gaze. Because I know about body language. I want him to think I'm meek. Scared.

The set of keys, along with a pistol, hangs on his belt. I eat the bread, careful to leave the dry crust.

Then I wait.

I wait for the moment I know will come.

I wait for him to get complacent.

When he drops his gaze, I attack. Quick as a flash, I shove the dry crust into his eye, and then push him to the ground. The muscles in my thighs are weak, but I clench them around the neck of the fucker who thinks he's going to shove a broom handle inside me. Not after what they did to Wolf. What they may be doing to Buck.

I squeeze.

I fucking squeeze.

I fucking squeeze the life out of him until I hear the crack of his bones. I let go, grab the keys and the pistol. Quickly I try the keys until I find the one that unlocks my cuffs. Then I peel the clothes off the guard's dead body, shove the sunglasses into the shirt pocket, and leave the foul-stenched cell.

No time to get dressed. I walk, still naked, until I find another guard. I shoot him through the head before he sees me, and when others come running to defense, I shoot them all too, until they're piled in a heap.

Then I search for Buck.

I unlock every door, staying as quiet as I can, until—

I find him. He's naked, on the ground, blood seeping from him. I place my hand on his neck.

He's alive.

"Buck!" I whisper harshly.

His eyes open.

"Come on. We're getting you out of here."

"How?"

"Friends on the inside. The guards have been...detained. We don't have much time."

He makes it to his feet. We always make it to our feet.

"Clothes?

"Waiting for us. Guards' clothes."

"Guards' clothes?"

The door to Buck's cell is open, and I pull him through it.

"Are you okay?" I ask.

"Fine," Buck groans. "Let's just get the fuck out of here."

I lead him to the pile of dead guards.

The other prisoners taunt us, but we pay them no mind.

They yell at us in foreign languages, sometimes in English. "Take us with you! Please!"

It hurts me to ignore their pleas, but I have no choice.

I'm on a mission, and the mission comes first.

"Come on. That one looks about your size." I gesture to one of the unconscious guards.

"Right." Buck gets to work undressing the guard.

I put on his clothing and take everything, including his firearms.

"Your eyes," Buck whispers.

"Already taken care of." I don the shades I took from the first guard.

Pain lances through me.

But I won't let any of it stop me.

They will not take me alive.

And they will not get any information out of me.

We stalk quietly through the pathways toward an open door, brandishing the guards' weapons.

"We may have to separate," I say.

Buck nods.

"Once we're out, get to safety. Anywhere. We'll find each other."

"The others?" Buck asks.

"Wolf didn't make it."

Footsteps advance toward us.

"See you on the outside," I turn right, while Buck goes left.

A moment later, a shot rings out.
Damn! Buck!
But I have no choice. I get out.
And I get out alive.
The Phoenix always rises.

37

KELLY

A buzzing.

The man who calls himself my father pulls out a phone.

"Damn," he says.

My so-called brother, The Dark One, glares at him. "What now?"

"I was right. They know we didn't leave the building. SWAT teams are on their way, and the building's on lockdown."

"Leif will come for me," I say.

"Leif won't get the chance," The Dark One says.

"You're no match for him."

The Dark One pulls a knife from the sheath at his waistband, holds it to my neck, the cool blade pressing against me. "If I can't have you, no one will."

"Cool it, Ronald," the elder Smith says. "No one's harming her."

"She's mine. You gave her to me."

"Right now our only option is Plan B."

"She won't make it."

"If we have to leave her here, Ronald, we will. We'll come back for her."

I don't know what they're talking about, but *please*, I beg the universe. *Please, let them leave me here. Leif will find me, and I'll be safe.*

Except...

Will I be? Will I ever be safe with the two of them out there?

"Did you know he plans to give his fortune to my mother and me?" I say, targeting The Dark One.

"Ronald knows I've already made adequate provisions for him."

"Besides, whatever you get will ultimately be mine," The Dark One says.

"Absolutely not. Do you think I'm going to share a penny with you?"

He places the blade at my neck once more. "You don't get it, do you Kelly? You're mine. You were always mine and you will always *be* mine."

"And you're a sick bastard," I say, waiting for his blade to slice me open.

I should be more scared than I am. But he never cut me on the island, although he threatened to. He raped me, but he never hurt me with the knife. I'm betting that he won't do so now.

"Get that knife off of her," Smith says. "You hurting her was never part of the deal."

"Hurting me wasn't part of the deal?" I can't help a stilted laugh. "You do know what he did to me on that island."

"He never harmed a hair on your head."

"You want to bet? I suppose you don't consider rape to be hurting a woman."

"You bear no scars from that," The Dark One says.

My father glares. "The place was a den of sin."

"You bet it was," I say, "so why did you send me there? If you're truly my father, you should've protected me."

"I shot my load into your mother some thirty years ago," he says. "That doesn't mean I have any feelings for you."

"Then why are you giving me your money? Why are you giving my mother your money?"

"I made a deal with your mother long ago," he says. "I made a deal...for you. All it took was a couple mill, and she was happy to tell me all about you and promise never to try to find you. She never knew about your brother, about how *he* felt about you, but I'm betting she would have gone with it if I'd thrown in a few diamonds."

"And you promised to give her all your money eventually? That doesn't make any sense."

"She's not getting a damned thing," Smith says. "But you are, Kelly."

"Why? I don't want your stupid money."

"Because...I'm old and tired and sick, and it's the least I can do."

"What?" I drop my jaw. "You're giving it to me out of *guilt*? That's a load of crap. If you had any guilt, you would never have—"

"Enough!" From Ronald. "Shut up. Just shut up."

I stop talking, but not because Ronald ordered me to. I stop talking because it's all coming together in my head.

It's a freaking horror story.

My mother...

My father...

And my half-brother...

Somehow they all found out about me, and Ronald—The Dark One—became obsessed with me.

My God, what a sick fuck.

My mother...

Oh, she was only too happy to sell me off.

And the server that day. Georgianna.

She must have been bought off too.

My God, is there anyone in the world who can't be bought?

Leif.

My Leif can't be bought.

"Both of you are a couple of sick fucks. And so is my fucking mother. She's a sow."

"Ronald, we need to execute the plan. Now."

"I'm not leaving without her."

"Fine, then," Smith says. "Stay here. Get caught. Spend the rest of your life in prison. When Derek Wolfe's kids uncovered that island, my money made your name go away. My money leaves with me."

"Pretty much what I thought," I can't help saying.

"If Ronald doesn't get any money, neither do you and your mother."

"Do I look like I care?" I cross my arms. "All I want is my life. My life with Leif."

"If you mention that name again," The Dark One grits out, "I will slice that milky throat open."

"Will you?" I close the distance between us and tilt my head, offering my neck. "Then do it. Just do it. Because I would rather die in a pool of my own blood than go anywhere with you."

"I'm leaving, Ronald," Smith says.

He walks toward a black duffel bag, pulls out ropes and some other equipment that I don't recognize.

He's going to scale the building. At his age? "Are you crazy?" I say.

"I won't be here long anyway," Smith says. "Ronald will fill you in."

"Like I'd believe anything he says." Not that I'd believe Smith either, for that matter.

"Fine, I'll go," The Dark One says, "but she's coming with us."

"Then you're responsible for her. You're on your own, Ronald. I'm out of here."

With haste, Smith gathers the rope, hooks himself into what looks like a canvas harness, and ties the rope off one of the pickets of cast iron railing on the balcony.

Smith has a shoulder holster. I noticed it earlier. He won't be able to use it, though. With a grunt, he hoists himself over the railing and begins his descent.

"Come on, Kelly," The Dark One says. "I'll harness you up."

"I'm not going anywhere with you."

"Do I need to remind you who has the knife?" He lifts his black hoodie. "And the gun?"

Indeed, a pistol is shoved into the waistband of his pants.

Chills rack my body, and my heart is beating double-time. But I refuse to show my fear.

"I told you. You're going to have to kill me."

"Don't think I won't."

"I'm pretty sure you will."

Except I don't think he will. His obsession with me runs deep.

"This can be easy," he says, "or it can be difficult."

"Make it easy, then. Why not just kill me and be done with it? If you don't leave soon, they will find you." I glance toward the balcony. "Your father's probably halfway down the building by now."

"Fuck my father."

"Of course that's what you would say. Once your father's dead, you get his money."

"Split three ways. Between you, me, and your mother."

"Great. You and Mommy dearest can squabble over my third. I'll be gone."

"You belong to me, so your third belongs to me. As far as I'm concerned, we're going to get your mother's money too."

"I'm her only next of kin, so when she dies, I'll get it anyway. Why the hurry?"

"Oh, Kelly. You have no idea who you're dealing with."

"I have a pretty good idea."

"You lived such a sheltered life."

Then I can't help myself. He's got a knife, and he's got a gun, and I still can't help myself. I burst out laughing.

"A sheltered life? You really don't know anything about me."

"Of course I do."

"From what source? My mother? She's a fucking liar. You're the one who lived a sheltered life, Ronald. What the hell is wrong with you, anyway? Your father has all kinds of money. You probably lived with a silver spoon in your mouth."

"Platinum, actually."

I laugh again. "You know what? You might as well slit my throat. You are such an asshole."

"Come on. It's time to go." He throws on a harness, and then he yanks me toward him, trying to get the harness on me. I stiffen, straight as a board.

"Damn it, Opal."

I freeze. Opal. That's what he called me on the island. Of course, that's what everyone called me on the island. But since he got in contact with me recently, he's always called me Kelly.

He straps the harness onto me. "We're going to go down together. You and I."

"I will not!"

"You will. Stop fighting me, Kelly."

I do my best, but The Dark One is stronger than I am, bigger than I am, and I'm still recovering from whatever they dosed me with. He eventually gets the harness on me, and he pulls me to him and straps us together. Then we go down over the balcony on the rope Smith already left there.

I don't look down. I can't. I squeeze my eyes shut. I'm not afraid of heights, but I *am* afraid of plummeting to my death.

We're strapped together, not unlike skydivers strap themselves together. The Dark One handles the rope, and we inch down slowly.

We're not as high up as I thought we were, but still, I'm so scared.

And then—

A gunshot.

One.

Two.

Three.

And...

A small screech as the rope begins to break.

Oh God oh God oh God...

Please...

Please... I told him to slit my throat, but I don't want to die.

I don't want to—

I scream as we plummet downward.

38

LEIF

I hate doing nothing.

With the building on lockdown, I can't even go outside.

So I pace. I pace across the marble floor of the ornate lobby, wondering who the hell designs hotel lobbies anyway. Why do they look like fucking French palaces? What's with the crystal chandelier and all the mirrors? It's a hotel, for God's sake.

Kelly. I have to protect Kelly.

But how?

I could—

I jerk as a gunshot rings out.

No. Not Kelly. I run toward the door. But I'm stopped by the police officers.

"I have to get to her." I push against them. "I have to!"

"Sir, you're not going anywhere."

Oh hell yes I am.

I break free, run to the entrance.

The doors are of course locked, so I can't go anywhere.

"Open the door," I say to the officer.

"Sir, I can't."

I grab him by the front of his uniform. "Open the door or I'm going to rearrange your face."

"First of all, you're not, and second, I literally can't. I don't have those codes. Only the chief of security does."

The chief of security...

Who may be in cahoots with—

I push the police officer aside and push at the emergency door. It opens.

Some security fucking chief.

"Sir, come back here!"

But I draw my gun, and I run.

I run toward the sound of the shot.

A few more shots ring out, and I pray that Kelly is not on the receiving end of them.

God, I'll never forgive myself for not protecting her.

I run around the side of the building, where the commotion is.

A body lies dead.

Then—

Two bodies drop from the building.

"Hurry!" SWAT members surround the bodies.

"Call 911, call 911!"

I push my way through.

"Sir, get back."

I draw my gun. "Fucking make me."

And then I see her.

I see my Kelly, her face pale and her eyes closed, on top of—

"Kelly!"

"Get back, sir!"

I trample through them all, determination willing me on, until I get to her.

I hold my hand to her neck.

Pulse. Thank God.

Whoever's beneath her broke her fall.

His head is cracked open, blood flowing out.

Kelly is harnessed to him.

I work at the harness.

"Sir, get back."

But Kelly's eyes flutter open then. "Leif?"

"I'm here, baby. I'm here."

"I knew you'd come for me..." Then her eyes close once again.

THE NEXT MORNING I sit in Kelly's hospital room, waiting for her to wake up.

Incredibly, she suffered no major injuries. No internal bleeding, no broken bones, not even a hairline fracture. No head damage. The doctors are calling it miraculous.

The man completely broke her fall.

He was dead at the scene, as was the other one—the one who got shot.

More questioning.

The cops are waiting outside to talk to Kelly, but I'm not allowing them near her.

Not until she's awake, fully alert.

The hospital is keeping her for observation for twenty-four hours at least, and I'm all for that. I'm not leaving her side.

The Wolfe family sent flowers, and I know Kelly will hate them.

They're putting together a memorial service for Brindley, even though she doesn't have any family. She has Kelly and me. She has Aspen and Buck and the other girls from the island. She has the Wolfe family.

Once Kelly is well and out of the hospital, we'll have the service.

A doctor enters the room. She takes a look at Kelly's chart. "Her vitals are looking great, and I'm getting good reports from the nurses."

I simply nod.

The doctor removes Kelly's covers and examines her abdomen.

"Everything still feels normal. I'm going to have her taken up to do another MRI later today just to make sure we didn't miss something in the first one. Sometimes internal bleeding or a brain bleed takes a while to show up."

My hearts jumps. "Are you concerned?"

"Not at all, but she did take quite a fall. She's lucky that the other man broke her fall."

"If not for that other man, she wouldn't have fallen in the first place."

The doctor nods. "Of course. You're right. I'll leave you two alone again. I'll be back during my evening rounds. In the meantime, if you need anything, check with the nurse and she'll page me if need be."

Again, I nod.

The doctors and the nurses have been great, and I'm so very grateful.

But I'm also feeling broken-down. I should have done better. I'm the one who was supposed to protect her.

So I stay with her.

I don't leave her side.

I will never leave her side again.

39

KELLY

Darkness.

The night is so dark. Must be a cloudy night. No stars. Not that I could see them. My eyes are squeezed shut. The Dark One seems handy with the rope as he scales down the walls of the building, hitting balcony after balcony.

Each time, I wonder how I could release myself from him and escape onto the balcony.

But we're hitched together with carabiners and canvas rope...

If only I could get to his gun or his knife. But then what would I do? Cut him? Shoot him? Then we both fall.

Leif is somewhere here.

He's close. If the police truly knew we were still in the building, then Leif knew too.

He's here somewhere. I have to believe he's going to come and rescue me.

Did Smith make it to the ground? I could look down, but I'm afraid to.

The rope tightens and moves with us, I don't know if it's from The Dark One or Smith.

But then—

A shot.

A gunshot. One...and then two or three more. Maybe more than that.

All I know is that one of them might have hit me.

I have no protection. Smith and The Dark One are probably wearing bulletproof clothing, but me?

No. I scream out.

The rope...It's breaking... The screech...

And then we're falling, falling, falling...

Time suspends itself.

What should take a microsecond actually takes moments... Hours even...

I wish...

I wish for life.

I wish for life with Leif.

But it's gone. Life can be gone in an instant. I didn't starve to death as a child, I didn't die from one of my mother's beatings, I didn't die on the island where I was tortured and abused.

I didn't die tonight when I told The Dark One to kill me. At least that would have been a dignified death, dying rather than going with him.

But this? Falling to the ground? No dignity in this death.

And now... This is no way for me to die. Strapped to The Dark One, the man I hate most in the world.

He's not my brother. Even if the DNA says he is...he's not. He's fucking not.

How is there time for me to be thinking all of this?

And then the drop...the pain...and the darkness.

40

LEIF

Kelly's eyelids are fluttering. She seems agitated, but she's asleep. A nightmare. I know the signs. I've been plagued by nightmares myself, and I've seen how Buck reacted while he was having one.

A nurse comes in.

"I'm glad you're here," I say to her. "She seems very disturbed."

"Her vitals are good, heart rate's up just a little. She's probably dreaming."

"It's not a dream. It's a nightmare."

"Some dreams are nightmares, Mr. Ramsey. I assure you she's fine."

"Could you give her something to calm her down?"

"Not without checking with her doctor."

"Could you check with her then?" I look at her face, at her clear agitation. It breaks my heart. "I don't want Kelly in any pain, physical or otherwise."

"When she wakes up, she won't remember any of this, Mr. Ramsey."

"But I can't bear the thought..." I rub my hand over my forehead.

"Medications are most likely contraindicated. She's already on antibiotics and analgesics. Something to calm her down will make her sleep more, and at this point, the doctors want her to wake up."

I nod. "I just..."

"She's been through a lot," the nurse says. "I understand your feelings. But everything looks good. The doctor seems to think she's going to pull through. She's lucky there are no lasting injuries."

"But she said—the doctor—that she wants to do another MRI."

"Yes, just to be sure. We don't take half measures here at this hospital, Mr. Ramsey. We want to make sure she's okay. And sometimes—"

"I know. Sometimes a slow bleed doesn't show up until twenty-four hours later."

That's not going to happen to Kelly. Damn it, it's not going to happen to Kelly.

The nurse makes some notes and then meets my gaze again. "Everything truly does look fine, Mr. Ramsey. Please try not to worry. If any of her vitals need my attention, an alarm will sound on her monitors."

"Yes, I know."

"So there's no reason for you to worry."

I sigh, grabbing Kelly's limp hand. "Not until we get the next MRI, anyway."

"I'm sure the doctor told you that she is confident things will be okay."

"Yes, but she can't guarantee anything."

"No doctor can, Mr. Ramsey. It would be unethical to make any kind of guarantee."

"I know."

I rub my forehead again. I'm sweating, but I'm cold. Worry consumes me. I can't lose Kelly. I just can't.

I hold onto her hand, listen to her heartbeat on the monitor. When her eyelids flutter, her heart rate increases. But not enough to set the alarms off.

Try not to worry, Mr. Ramsey.

Funny. All those times overseas when my life was truly in peril—when I watched my friends die—I didn't worry like this. I was concerned. I did what I had to do to save my life and others. And I wasn't always successful.

But it was my job, and I did it to the best of my ability.

And somehow... Somehow I always rose from the ashes.

But I'm not the person who concerns me now. Kelly is. I want *her* to be the Phoenix. I want *her* to rise.

She's strong. Strong and determined.

Still...worry eats at my gut.

I sit, holding her hand, trying to pour all my energy into her.

I'm not sure how many moments pass—probably over an hour—before someone enters.

It's a new nurse. She's wearing blue scrubs, like the other nurse, but something's different.

"How is she doing?" the nurse asks.

"The same. What happened to Felicity?"

"Her shift is over," this nurse says. "My name is Hope."

Hope.

Good name. That's what I need to have. Hope. It was damned hard in Afghanistan to keep hold of hope, but we did. Buck and I both. Even the others—Wolf, Ace, Ghost, Eagle. They all had hope until their dying breath.

You have to have hope. You have to have strength. You have to have such mental fortitude that you can't even imagine weakness.

I try to hold onto that now.

That mental fortitude.

That hope.

Hope holds up an IV bag.

"Is that medication? Did you decide to give her something for her agitation?"

"Yes."

"So you checked with the doctor, and she said it was okay?"

"Absolutely. We don't want this patient to be in any undue distress."

Thank God. At least Kelly will have some peace. Although I wish she would wake up.

"How long will it take for this medication to take effect?"

"Not too long, Mister...."

"Ramsey. Good."

I wipe my hand over my forehead again. Such a cold sweat. How come she doesn't know my name? It's all over the records. Oh, well. It's the beginning of her shift. Maybe she didn't notice my name.

Hope hangs the bag of medication, attaches it to Kelly's IV, and then leaves.

A moment later, Felicity enters. "Time to check—"

I stand, letting go of Kelly's hand. "I thought your shift was over."

"No. I'm on for another few hours. Let's check her—"

I yank Kelly's IV out of her arm. Alarms begin blaring as blood trickles from the IV site.

"Mr. Ramsey? What are you doing?"

"Another nurse came in. A nurse named Hope. Do you know her?"

Her eyes widen. "No, I don't."

"She said the doctor had changed his mind about some sedation for Kelly. She hung that bag up on the IV and added it."

"Oh my God," Felicity looks at the bag. "It's unmarked, but not much has gone into her. We'll get it down to the lab right away."

"What about Kelly? We have to wake her."

"We'll get some labs right away. Toxicology. Stat."

With the alarms still blaring, seconds later, another nurse comes to draw Kelly's blood.

God, Kelly. No.

A man in the same blue scrubs hurries in. "I'm Zeb, the charge nurse. I'm so sorry—"

"What the hell happened?" I demand. "How could you people let some imposter in here?"

"I'm so sorry," the charge nurse says. "We're going to make sure she gets the best care. You're going to have to leave, Mr. Ramsey."

"I'm not leaving her side."

"You're going to have to. I'm so sorry, but we need to take all precautions. She probably didn't get enough of anything into her IV to do any lasting harm, but we can't take that chance. We're going to have to pump her."

"Oh my God..."

"Mr. Ramsey," Zeb says. "Please."

And I leave.

I leave because it's what's best for Kelly, but only because it's what's best for Kelly. If I had it my way I'd be standing over all of them, asking for credentials and making sure they're on the right shift.

I walk to the end of the hallway to the small waiting area on this floor and pace across it. For hours. Fucking hours.

It's forever until I finally get word.

Felicity comes to find me. "Mr. Ramsey, she's okay now. Toxicology came back negative. She's a lucky woman. That bag contained two grams of sodium pentothal. If she had…"

She stops. She doesn't have to say more. I know what could have—most likely would have—happened.

"Mr. Ramsey, you saved her life today. She's awake, and she's asking for you."

41

KELLY

Leif.

My vision is still blurry, but he looks wonderful. Like an angel, a halo around him and everything.

I know it's just my blurred vision, my brain playing tricks on me, but I'm going with it.

"Kelly..." He grabs my hand, kisses my cheek. "Thank God."

"What happened?" I ask.

"They didn't tell you?"

"Not really. Lots of gobbledygook. The last thing I remember is"— *The rope...it's breaking... The screech... And then we're falling, falling, falling*— "God. Falling."

"Yes. You fell from the side of the hotel. You were strapped to someone and he broke your fall."

"The Dark One..."

"It was him? Your father?"

"No..." A shudder surges through me. "He said he was... my brother."

"Brother? What?"

"It's... A lot to tell you."

"Shh." He kisses my cheek. "You rest. You can tell me everything later. I love you."

"I love you too."

"Mr. Ramsey?" A nurse asks.

"Yeah, what is it?"

"The police need to talk to you. About whoever tried to poison Ms. Taylor."

Poison? Someone tried to poison me? My eyes fall closed.

"They're going to have to wait. I'm not leaving her side."

"All right. I'll tell them."

An officer appears at the door of my room. "Mr. Ramsey, I understand your hesitancy to leave her, but we need to get your statement while it's still fresh in your mind."

"Trust me, Officer, I will never forget."

"If it's all the same—"

I open my eyes and squeeze his hand. At least I think I do. My body isn't working quite right just yet. "Please, Leif. Go ahead. I want whoever is behind all of this to pay."

"All right." He kisses my forehead. "I do too, baby. But we will be right outside the door, and I will keep my eye on you the entire time."

I nod and let my eyes flutter closed.

Leif saved me today. I always knew he'd come for me.

I always knew he would.

A FEW HOURS LATER, my eyes open and Leif is next to me again.

"Hey you. Good news. While you were asleep, they took you for another MRI, and everything looks good."

"I had an MRI?"

"Yes, one when you first came in, which was clear. It's pretty amazing. No internal bleeding, including in your brain. You survived that fall because the other guy broke it."

"What happened to him?"

"Dead on impact. The police think he probably had a fail-safe in place. If something happened to him, he had someone ready to come in and poison you."

"Poison me. So I heard you right. I heard the nurse right. Why would he…"

"Because he was a sick man, Kelly. I don't know if he was your brother or not. And I don't know if Forester Smith was your father either, but if you consent, we can do a DNA test to find out."

I shake my head, the strain making me ache. "I don't want to know. Don't do the DNA test. They're both dead now, so what does it matter?"

"I understand. I wouldn't want to know if I were related to such sick fucks either."

"Right."

"The good news is, your doctor says if you continue to improve, I can take you home in a few days."

"I want to go home."

"When I say home, I mean home to my place. Because that's where you're going to live from now on."

"You mean?"

"Of course I do. I love you, Kelly. I'm never letting you out of my sight again."

"You saved my life."

"Maybe at the end, but if I hadn't taken you with me to the hotel—"

"He would've found me, Leif. I don't know how, but he would have. He was obsessed. My brother—The Dark One—was obsessed with me. I... It's a long story. It's all so sick and twisted."

"It is, and you can tell me everything after you're well rested. You're safe now. The two of them are gone. Forever."

A feeling of utter calm—something I've never experienced before—swaths me. They're gone.

"But it came at a price," I say.

"It did. Brindley."

"How can I ever forgive myself for that?"

"You have to. You apologized to her for treating her badly, and you meant it. She believed you. She went to her grave knowing you were friends."

"But it's because of me that—"

He places two fingers over my lips. "Please, Kelly. Don't go there. I've been there, and it's not a pretty place. Don't blame yourself. It wasn't your fault."

Yes, Leif has been there. Friends who never came home. Friends who he was supposed to save but couldn't.

The situations aren't identical, but they're close.

"How? How do I move past it?"

"You just do, Kelly. You make a conscious choice. Others may have died, but you lived. Make that life worthwhile. Make sure they did not die in vain."

42

LEIF

wo weeks later...

"It was a lovely service for Brindley," Aspen says.

"How is your mom doing?" I ask.

"She's good. She thought it was important that Buck and I come back for the service."

"Plus, we wanted to," Buck says. "Did Reid tell you they tracked down the security guards who went missing? They were found locked in a safe house upstate."

"Yeah, he told me. I'm glad they're going to be okay."

"How's Kelly doing?" Aspen asks.

I gaze at Kelly. She's still sitting in the small chapel where the Wolfes arranged the service. Attendance was small, of course. Kelly and me, Buck and Aspen. Rock and Lacey, Reid and Zee, Macy, and some other Wolfe employees.

The other girls who still live in town—Marianne, Francine, and Lily.

The Wolfes arranged a small wake at Reid and Zee's.

Buck, Aspen, Kelly, and I are the only ones still here at the chapel.

Kelly still sits in the front row, staring at the photograph of Brindley on display and the urn containing her ashes.

"She's taking it so hard," I say.

"We all are," Aspen says, "but Kelly... She's been through so much."

Buck nods. "She'll be okay. She's strong."

"She is," Aspen agrees. "We all are. We had to be to survive. That island would've eaten us up otherwise."

"It's amazing most of you came out mentally healthy," Buck says.

Aspen smiles. "We can thank the Wolfes for that. That retreat center they built on the island saved us. Without that intensive treatment, I don't think we'd have had such good results."

"I'm going to see if she's ready." I walk back into the chapel. "Baby?"

She looks up at me, her eyes red and swollen from crying.

"You ready?"

Kelly gazes at the pewter urn. "I don't want to leave her. She's alone."

"She's not alone. Not anymore. Come on."

"Leif...how can you and I go on? How can we allow ourselves to be happy when Brindley died such a horrible death? All because of me?"

"Because it's what Brindley would have wanted, Kelly. Just like it's what Wolf and Ghost and the others wanted for me and for Buck. They didn't get the chance at life, but we did. We have that chance, and we would be doing them all a disservice if we didn't take it. If we didn't vow to live our best lives, to be happy."

"I just feel so much guilt."

"I understand, baby. Believe me."

She nods. "I do believe you, Leif. I'm so sorry for what you've been through."

"I'm sorry for what you've been through, Kelly. But our pasts don't define us. We make the present that we want. The future that we want."

She nods and rises. She walks toward Brindley's urn, trails her fingers over it. "Goodbye, Brindley. Wherever you are, I'm glad you're finally at peace." She turns. "I'm ready."

Buck and Aspen are waiting for us in the small narthex, and Kelly and I walk down the aisle of the tiny chapel.

Before we get to Buck and Aspen, a young man waylays us out of nowhere. "Are you Ms. Kelly Taylor?" he asks.

"Yes."

"I'm Fred Stein." He hands Kelly a card.

"You're an attorney?"

"Yes, ma'am. I represent the estate of Forrester Smith. You are his soul heir and beneficiary, according to his last will."

Kelly drops her jaw.

"We'll have a reading of the will tomorrow morning at nine a.m., my office. You should be there."

"I don't understand."

"Apparently he wasn't lying to you," I say. "He *did* leave you his millions."

"Quite a few millions at that," Stein says.

"What about my mother?"

"What about her?"

"He said he was leaving it to both of us."

"You're the only one mentioned. You and his son, Ronald Smith. But Ronald Smith is dead and left no heirs, so it all goes to you, Ms. Taylor."

She says nothing.

"You're going to be a rich woman, Ms. Taylor. To the tune of a little less than nine hundred million."

Kelly sways, but I steady her.

"You're kidding me," she says.

"I'm not kidding. Be there tomorrow, and we'll get things moving through probate."

"Mr. Stein?" I say.

"Yes?"

"This money that Mr. Smith left for Kelly." I step closer to him and lower my voice. "Is it...legitimate money? I mean not laundered money?"

"I can't make any opinion as to where the money originated. But this is generational wealth, Mister..."

"Ramsey. Leif Ramsey. I'm Kelly's...fiancé."

Kelly looks up at me, her eyes questioning. Then she smiles.

"Generational wealth?" I say. "He said he made his money in foreign currency."

"He may have made some money there," Mr. Stein says, "but the bulk of his wealth is generational. Mr. Smith was a member of the Hilton family."

"Hilton Hotels?" I drop my jaw.

"No. Hilton copper."

"I didn't realize there was so much money in copper."

"Copper is used for a lot of technology," Stein says, "and you, Ms. Taylor, are a very wealthy woman."

Kelly swallows. "I don't want it. My father—Mr. Smith—he claims he was my father—was not a good man."

"Be that as it may," Stein says, "you are the sole beneficiary to his estate. If you don't want it, you can give it all to charity. But it is yours, and I do need you to be there tomorrow morning."

"We'll be there," I say.

Kelly leans against me.

Once Stein leaves, she looks up at me. "Fiancée? You want to marry me?"

"Yes, I do, Kelly." I grin. "And not just for your money."

She grimaces. "Good, because I'm giving it all away."

"It's yours, baby. You can do whatever you want with it. Come on. Let's go to the wake. We'll send Brindley off in style."

43

KELLY

"What do you mean there's no provision for me?" My mother stands, advancing toward Mr. Stein at the head of the small conference room table.

"You have the document in front of you, Ms. Taylor. The only two mentioned in the will are your daughter and Ronald Smith. Since Mr. Smith is deceased and left no heirs, everything goes to your daughter."

My mother slams her hand down on the table. "But he promised me. He promised me it would be divided between Kelly and me."

"Apparently he lied."

"I'll contest it."

"Contest it all you want. But you'll lose, and you'll end up just having spent your money on attorneys' fees."

My mother turns to me then. "You'll split it with me, won't you Kelly?"

I scoff. "You're kidding, right?"

"I'm your mother."

I rise and meet my mother's gaze. "Only by DNA. You were never a mother to me. You forced me to grow up when I was just a child. I was responsible for making meals when I was eight years old. Scrounging for food in our bare kitchen. What time I didn't spend going to school or working around the house, I spent in the closet—locked in there by you. In complete and cold darkness. When I finally found something that made me happy—volleyball—you took that away. You kicked me out of the house when I turned eighteen. The middle of my senior year, Mom. I had nowhere to go, and I'm just lucky that someone took me in. So no... I'm not giving you any of the money."

"What on earth are you going to do with nine hundred million dollars?"

"I'll keep a little of it, so Leif and I can get started out in life. But most of it? It's going to charity. I'm going to start a foundation. The Brindley McGregor Foundation to help young adults who have grown up in the system and have nowhere to go. The rest of it will go to the Wolfe Retreat Center on the island."

"The Wolfes don't need your charity."

"No, they don't. But the men and women who go to the retreat center do. I want to help them. I'm lucky I got the help I did. It's only because of that therapy that I learned I'm a worthy human being, Mother. I certainly never learned that from you."

Mr. Stein clears his throat. "I'm filing the papers with probate court today," he says. "As Mr. Smith's attorney and personal representative, I have the authority to act on behalf of the estate. Kelly, I'm going to need your signature on several of these papers."

"When does she get the money?" my mother asks.

"What business of that is yours?" Leif says.

"Kelly, I'm going to expedite probate as best I can. It shouldn't take longer than three months. Six months at the most. Mr. Smith liquidated most of his assets in the last year, so there's no issue of real property. It's all cash, Kelly. Liquid cash."

"I just can't believe it," I say. "I'm not even sure he *is* my father."

"You can still have that DNA test," Leif says.

"No." Then I look to Mr. Stein. "That doesn't matter, does it?"

"No. You're the beneficiary, whether you're related or not."

"But he does say in the will that he leaves his estate to his daughter, Kelly Taylor."

"He believes you to be his daughter. That's good enough for the courts and that's good enough for me. The DNA test isn't required."

"Maybe *I'll* require it," my mother says.

"For God's sake." Leif rolls his eyes.

"It's not really your place to require anything, Ms. Taylor," Stein says. "You're not a beneficiary. The will says what it says. DNA is not required to satisfy the terms of the will or to satisfy the probate court."

"I'd like to know. Kelly, wouldn't you like to know? Find out if you descended from that psycho?"

"I'm already descended from one psycho," I say. "I think I'll stay ignorant of the rest."

"Here are the papers," Stein says. "Just sign where I've put the tabs."

"Should I have an attorney look at these?" I ask Leif.

259

"No. I think if you and I read through them it's good enough. I mean, like Mr. Stein said, the will says what it says. The money is yours, Kelly. Yours to do with what you want."

I grab Leif's hands. "Do you want me to keep all of it? I mean, we'd be set for life, Leif. Any children that we have would be set for life, and their children…"

"Baby, that's up to you. If you want to start a charity in Brindley's name and give the rest to the retreat center, I think that's wonderful."

"I'll keep enough so we can build a nice house. Get started on both feet."

"Whatever you want," he says. "I'm behind you a hundred percent."

I scan the documents, ask Mr. Stein to clarify a few things, and then I sign.

"Good enough," Mr. Stein says. "I'll be in touch. In the meantime, Ms. Taylor, enjoy your life."

I smile. "Thank you, Mr. Stein. I will."

EPILOGUE
LEIF

True to his word, Mr. Stein got everything expedited, and within three months, Kelly was a very rich woman.

True to *her* word, she kept ten million dollars of the money and then founded The Brindley McGregor Foundation and hired a competent staff to get it off the ground. The remainder went to the Wolfe Retreat Center to help women like herself.

"I wish Brindley had family," she says. "I'd happily give them some of this money as well."

"I know, baby. But you're helping a lot of people like her, and Brindley, wherever she is, is smiling down at you. She's happy for you, happy for us. So let's give her something to be happy about."

"What kind of house do you want?" she asks.

I pause a moment, thinking about Texas. My home. "What do you think about a sprawling ranch house?"

She laughs. "In Manhattan? I think that's out of the question."

"How about in Summer Creek, Texas?" I ask.

"Your hometown?"

"Yeah, my hometown. My dad always wanted me to come back, learn the ranching business. What do you say?"

"I don't really see myself as a ranch wife."

"All right, if it's not what you want, we'll do something else. We can go anywhere, Kelly. Anywhere. You just tell me where."

"How about…Summer Creek, Texas." She smiles.

"You changed your mind about being a ranch wife already?"

"No. But we have ten million dollars. I'll be able to pay someone to do the cooking and cleaning." She chuckles. "I'm kidding. Well, only half kidding. I know how to cook, and I do love animals. Maybe I'd be good on a ranch."

"Baby, you'll be good wherever you go. But only if it's what you want."

She links her arm through mine. "I think it is, Leif."

"Tell you what. Why don't we try it out? Because I do have to go home. For a little while, at least."

"Oh?"

"Yes. I need to see an old friend."

"Of course. Whatever you need. What old friend?"

I haven't told Kelly about Falcon Bellamy. About how he went to prison, and how he's getting released.

Next week.

My father called me yesterday. He gets out next week.

I need to be there.

I need to find out the truth.

Because I never thought Falcon Bellamy was a criminal.

"His name is Falcon."

"That's an unusual name."

"Yeah. He has two brothers, Hawk and Eagle. And two sisters, Robin and Raven. His mother's name is Starling."

"What's his father's name? Vulture?"

I chuckle. "His father's name is Austin. Austin Bellamy."

Her eyes widen. "I think I've heard that name."

"Yeah. He's the son of Brick Bellamy and Sandra Cooper —the steel heiress."

"Why haven't I heard of their kids?"

"Because...they laid out a lot of money to keep the current scandal quiet."

"Current scandal?"

I clear my throat. "Falcon Bellamy was my best friend growing up. We were supposed to join the Navy together after college, but he...got into some trouble."

"What kind of trouble?"

I draw in a deep breath.

And then I begin.

LEARN about Falcon Bellamy in *Savage Sin*, coming soon!

SAVAGE SIN TEASER

The place is a dive.

Funny.

Before, I'd never have considered entering such a bar, but now?

Now, I'm different.

I've seen how the other half lives.

I've been part of the other half.

And this dive? It called to me, so I went in.

The bar stools are covered in red vinyl, and the one I choose has a couple of rips in it. Seems appropriate. It's early —only eight p.m.—so there's no crowd yet, if there ever is one. Maybe these old bars on the edge of towns don't do much business. Not that I'd know.

A neon *Old Milwaukee* sign hangs on the wall behind the bar, above the shelves of bottles with names I don't recognize. Probably all rotgut.

I'm not used to rotgut, but nearly a decade has passed since I've tasted alcohol that wasn't fermented in a toilet tank, so I'm pretty sure the well brands here will taste like fucking Pappy's.

No one else sits at the bar, but the barkeep on duty—a middle-aged woman who seems intent on wiping lowball glasses—doesn't seem in any hurry to offer me a libation.

I clear my throat. "Ma'am?"

"Be with you in a minute," she says, her voice low and raspy. A smoker, no doubt.

A couple tables are occupied with young men wearing T-shirts and orange vests. Construction workers, probably, just getting off duty. In the background, headbanger music plays softly over the intercom. Ironic. An old juke sits in one corner, but it's not lit. Probably just for show. The tables and the bar are crafted from some kind of dark wood. The bar itself is full of scratches and needs revarnishing.

"What'll it be?" the barkeep finally says to me.

"Bourbon. Neat."

"You got it. Brand?"

"The shittiest you've got."

She laughs, and it sounds kind of like a frog croaking. "Been that kind of day, huh?"

I look down at the scratched surface of the bar. "You don't even know."

She turns, grabs a bottle without a label, and pours a shot into a lowball glass.

"Better make it a double," I say.

"You got it."

She adds another fingerful and slides the glass to me, along with a napkin that says "Ruthie's Roadies" on it.

"You Ruthie?" I ask.

Another low laugh. "Hell, no. I'm Iris. We get these

266

napkins at a discount. Buy up leftover stock from other places."

"Ah. Got it." I pick up the glass. Take a sniff. Whew! Harsh stuff. A little woodsy, a touch of caramel, and a whole lot of battery acid.

"What's your name, cowboy?" Iris asks.

I raise an eyebrow. "Do I look like a cowboy to you?"

She eyes the tats on my knuckles. My shaggy dark hair that nearly touches my shoulders. My black stubble. "Not so much. What are you, then?"

"Not sure." I shoot the bourbon, letting it crawl down my throat in a slow burn. I slide the glass back to her. "One more."

She nods, pours me a refill, and hands it back. "You going to tell me your name?"

I hold up my glass, swirl the light brown liquid in the glass, the way I used to swirl wine. I used to appreciate fine wine. My mother taught me about wine when I was sixteen years old. She loves the stuff, used to have it shipped from Napa Valley, Burgundy, Tuscany—you name it—to our Summer Creek, Texas ranch. I enjoyed the stuff, and not just because I was only sixteen and it was a thrill to drink. No. I enjoyed the nuances, the colors and aromas, the flavor as it trickled over my tongue and then the finish as I swallowed. Mom said I had the same knack for wine that she did. We talked about going to Europe on a wine tour once I finished college. We'd planned to do it after graduation and before I joined the Navy with my best friend, Leif.

None of that happened, of course.

It couldn't.

I polish off the second drink and exhale. "It's Falcon."

"Say what?"

"You asked my name. It's Falcon."

"You're shittin' me."

"Nope. I'd show you my driver's license, except I have to get a new one."

Iris frowns. "No driver's license? Good thing I didn't ID you. How'd you get here?"

"Cab."

"Yeah? What have you been doin'?"

I push the glass toward her, motioning for another. "Time."

A NOTE FROM HELEN

Dear Reader,

Thank you for reading *Phoenix*. If you want to find out about my current backlist and future releases, please visit my website, like my Facebook page, and join my mailing list. If you're a fan, please join my Facebook street team (Hardt & Soul) to help spread the word about my books. I regularly do awesome giveaways for my street team members.

If you enjoyed the story, please take the time to leave a review. I welcome all feedback.

I wish you all the best!

Helen

Sign up for my newsletter here:

http://www.helenhardt.com/signup

ACKNOWLEDGMENTS

Thank you so much to the following individuals who helped make this story shine: My editor (and son!), Eric McConnell, my cover artists, Kim Killion and Amanda Shepard, and my awesome beta readers, Karen Aguilera, Serena Drummond, Linda Dunn, and Angela Tyler. You all rock!

ALSO BY HELEN HARDT

My Heart Still Beats

Bellamy Brothers

Savage Sin

Sweet Sin

Seductive Sin

Follow Me Series

Follow Me Darkly

Follow Me Under

Follow Me Always

Darkly

Under

Black Rose Series

Blush

Bloom

Blossom

Wolfes of Manhattan

Rebel

Recluse

Runaway

Rake

ABOUT THE AUTHOR

#1 *New York Times*, #1 *USA Today*, and #1 *Wall Street Journal* bestselling author Helen Hardt's passion for the written word began with the books her mother read to her at bedtime. She wrote her first story at age six and hasn't stopped since. In addition to being an award-winning author of romantic fiction, she's a mother, an attorney, a black belt in Taekwondo, a grammar geek, an appreciator of fine red wine, and a lover of Ben and Jerry's ice cream. She writes from her home in Colorado, where she lives with her family. Helen loves to hear from readers.

Please sign up for her newsletter here:
http://www.helenhardt.com/signup
Visit her here:
http://www.helenhardt.com

Printed in Great Britain
by Amazon

45852834R00169